Guardian Angels Come in

This Dog's Afterlife

Book 1

By
David S. Shockley II

For

Goldfinger
Lily, Chanook, Bo, Morris, Sampson, Lucky, Peaches,
Princess, Duncan, Louie, Abby, Chili, Kaleb, Rumor, Effrom
Blue, Shiloh, Lil Maw, Samson, Squeaky
&
Buddy

May you find endless bones to bury, infinite spots to snuggle,
and countless balls to chase!

~Dave~

1
<u>The End</u>

My name is Tucker, and the last few months of my life were no fun at all. I feel it's important to make this fact very clear, very early. Where my time was concerned, Captain Fun had finished his performance, bid adieu, and promptly exited stage right. He gave no hints of an encore, there were no autographs for his adoring fans—he simply smiled, bowed, winked to the masses, and departed.

The end came on a Wednesday in May, and let me assure you, it could not have been a more flawless day. For starters, the weather was impeccable. The sun was an intense but tender shade of gold, and there were only a handful of cheerful clouds in the sky. Those that did drift by were a brilliant pearly white and appeared to emit their own warm glow. The sky was as blue as I'd ever seen it, a perfect cobalt backdrop to the playful clouds. It had rained for most of the week prior, coaxing the grass into a rich, dark jade, and almost every tree was in a full, eager bloom. The windows in the house stood open, allowing you to smell and hear everything outside, the aromas thick and staggering.

I spent nearly the entire morning watching my brother Chanook race about in the yard, as all dogs should in such weather. He chased squirrels he knew would always evade him. He rolled in whatever scent inspired him, and he barked hello to the golfers that strolled by on their endless search for tiny lost balls. Yes, it was a magnificent day indeed.

But as lovely as the weather was, I was unable to take pleasure in it the way I wanted to, the way a day like that really *should* be enjoyed. On that day, there would be no running through the grass. There would be no walk or a leisurely roll in the leaves—not anymore. That Captain Fun gent I was referring to? Well, after his departure, what little cartilage remained in my hips followed suit. So for the last few months I was around, let's just say I found a new friend, and he was a bit of a…excuse the language…but he was a bastard of the highest pedigree. This new chap went by the name of Pain. And to say that he was a pain in the rump would not be far from the truth. Lord, how I despised him.

Despite the borderline agony I was struggling with and the heart-wrenching desire to dash about outdoors, that last day in May was actually a wonderful one. You see, right around noon, when the sun was highest in the sky and the birds were singing their best, I was finally able to get on with my life—well, *afterlife*, anyway. For the first time in many a month I began living again, in a manner of speaking.

I remember it happened quickly, and I recall the scent of sadness drifting about the family beforehand. Heartache has a very unique aroma, and that day it permeated everything. It wove its way into the furniture, the carpet, and my home's very walls. From the moment I woke that morning until the instant my pain finally vanished, the entire family seemed to be crying on the inside. Sorrow's scent is a perfume I'd gladly forget if I could.

For as long as I can remember, I have been loved. Never was I without food or shelter. Not once did my various injuries go untreated, and never was I abused. So on this wonderful day in May, things were no different. The doctor who came to the house that afternoon was new to me, but I liked him right away. He smiled at my family and towards my brother; he even scratched us both behind the ears. He spoke in a tender tone, and a scent of kindness radiated from him. There were a few awkward moments amongst the family, and then almost everyone gathered around where I lay. I was too weak and in too much pain to go much further than my bed. My owner Dave took Chanook to the back of the house, and I could hear his comforting words gliding down the hallways and through the rooms. There was a small pinch, the pain vanished, and blissful sleep overtook me. The last thing I remember was my owner Rebecca holding me and rubbing my head. It was magnificent.

~

When I opened my eyes again, nothing had changed, yet everything was different. The house seemed larger and far livelier in an ironic sort of way. Colors were more vibrant than I recalled; many were new to me. The aromas that drifted about were more pungent than ever. Each sound seemed to be amplified by crystals and diamonds.

My favorite discovery was my new ability to not only hear but to understand my owners—and not just their language, but their thoughts as well! I somehow knew they could no longer see me, but strangely enough, I was unbothered by it, as if it was simply a new and understood fact which I readily accepted. I immediately understood that we would meet again someday, but until then, I would just have to make do. I wasn't sure how I knew that, or how I could fathom the things I suddenly did, but it was a comforting feeling. I felt young again, alive again, and I wanted to run, jump, and play again—so I did.

2
<u>The Things One Learns</u>

Let's talk about death for a minute, shall we? Or rather, my death, considering it's the one I'm most familiar with. To start, I'd like to say mine wasn't half-bad! I realize that's not the case for many, but mine was actually quite nice, like going to sleep with the promise of spring in the morning. With the exception of a sudden tragic loss, or the passing of a far too young soul, the unhappiness surrounding the ordeal made little sense to me at the time. I had no inkling that it was such a mystery to so many, especially humans. Personally, I'd always known there was something else waiting for me after I died. I knew there would always be another life to live, a new and better place to explore and enjoy. My heart goes out to those who don't believe in such a thing, or are simply unaware. It must be a terrifying prospect, the idea that in an instant you know no more.

When it was my turn to experience this event, the first thing that I encountered was a potent, almost overwhelming avalanche of mental awareness. I was inundated with magnificent, vast amounts of knowledge. And I began to understand things that I'd never even imagined as possible—strange, wonderful things. It was as if somewhere in the back of my mind a tiny dial had been turned. A dial which allowed me access to information which I'd once known, but for one reason or another, I'd forgotten.

I was also acutely aware that there was far, far more to learn, and that someone close to me was coming to help with quite a bit of it. I wasn't entirely sure who it was going to be, but I had a guess. I knew it was someone important to me, or at least they *had* been, so that narrowed the field considerably. In the meantime, I mulled over my new understandings, my freshly acquired knowledge. For instance, I could listen to my family's thoughts, as I mentioned earlier. I realized that I could communicate my feelings to them even though I was gone. I wasn't entirely sure on how to go about doing so, but I did understand that it was possible. I was also aware that we were closer now than ever before. I know that sounds counterintuitive and I attest that at the time I was a little baffled by it as well, but I would understand more in short order.

Another important fact I soon realized was that I could now comprehend the sorrow and pain humans experience over the loss of a loved one. This was a novel concept for me, but the weight of it insisted I not only take notice, but pay close attention to its significance. The majority of this grief revolves around their obsession with and perception of time (but I'll talk more about that later). I began to realize that humans rarely see the ones they've lost until they shuffle off their own mortal coil. This was never an issue for me. As far as I was aware, it had never been an issue for anyone else I'd known during my life. And by anyone, I mean the other animals I'd known.

When I was a pup, it took me weeks to understand why my owners never seemed to notice my father. I mean he was right there, all the time, and he was a rambunctious fellow, always far more excited than any given occasion called for. He slept in the middle of the room, on the furniture, even on the beds throughout the house. He ate copious amounts of food which he somehow managed to take from the refrigerator, howled whenever inspiration struck, and reveled in plodding through mud and dirt only to track it indoors and onto, well, everything. He was not easily ignored, yet my owners did just that, with no effort at all. He told me his name was Rocket, and when I was almost a year old, he informed me that he'd died just after I was born in an unfortunate incident involving a car and an undeniable fixation he had at the time regarding automotive tires, especially when they were spinning.

"At least it was painless!" he'd said. "And quick; almost caught her too!" he had added with a tangible sense of regret. He was then quick to instruct me never to play in the street when I grew older.

And that's when I began to understand why my owners never appeared to notice my father. He was a ghost, a spirit, a phantom in their midst. I assumed at the time that as I could see Rocket and they could not, there were spirits they could perceive and likewise I could not. It wasn't until I'd crossed over myself that I understood how very rare it was for humans to perceive such entities when they were present.

Rocket also informed me that he wasn't permitted to say very much about the things that happen after one dies. There were rules, you see, and there was someone pretty important who'd asked Rocket to follow them—which he did without hesitation. My father couldn't answer many of my questions (trust me, there were multitudes of them) and it wasn't until I passed on myself that I learned the answers I'd wanted to know so much before. On my first birthday, Rocket bid farewell, and just like that, he vanished.

4

And that's how it was with me that sunny day in May. My owners had no idea I was there. In fact, they packed up a few belongings, put a leash on Chanook, and headed off to enjoy the splendid weather. I sensed that more than anything, they were trying to shed some of the sorrow following my death, as if the house needed to air out. Perhaps that was why all of the windows were open. Rebecca was devastated, and I felt immediately responsible, as if I should have done something to prevent my own death; silly, I know. Yet I still felt I was to blame for her sadness. It wasn't until Rocket arrived that I learned I could go with them if I wished...and when I say "arrived," I mean he literally appeared right beside me.

"So are you ready for all of those answers, kiddo?"

Have you ever been startled, I mean REALLY startled? Only to see who it was that frightened you and then burst out laughing? That is precisely what I did. "Rocket!"

We circled about, happy to see one another after so many years. I have to admit, he had faded from my memory quite a bit, but seeing my father standing in the living room again brought back all my childhood memories of him. *And* he looked exactly the same: his fur was still a shadowy black with bits of butterscotch, his eyes were as blue as ever, and his whiskers were still a tad bit gray.

"Where have you been all of this time?" I asked. "It's been what, a decade or more?"

"I've been near. I stop in every now and then to check on you and Chanook. That kid's a character, isn't he?"

That conjured a rather large smile and a good chuckle. "Yes, he is."

Rocket walked over to Chanook's bed and sniffed. "I haven't met his parents yet, but I've heard stories of his father. He's evidently something of a car enthusiast himself!"

"Well, why didn't you ever stop by and say hello?" I asked. "I'd almost forgotten about you. That just seems wrong somehow."

Rocket sighed and looked out the window at several golfers searching the backyard for another lost ball. "There are a few thoughts on remaining with your family for too long after you've passed. Something about the living and their lives etcetera, etcetera. So I just kind of hung out in the wings and looked over you from the shadows."

"Well, that's a bit...creepy."

5

Rocket chuckled. "I guess it is, in a way. I have to admit I spooked Nook a few times just to see what he'd do."

"And what *did* he do?"

"Exactly what I figured he would: he'd chase shadows for a while, and generally look confused."

"He excels at looking confused."

Rocket laughed. "He sure does!"

My father then turned his attention from the backyard and made his way into the kitchen. I followed and watched in awe as he poked his head *through* the refrigerator door, sniffed about, and withdrew with a brightly colored orange.

"So THAT'S how you always did that when I was a pup!"

"Yep! Best part is, no one ever knows! Wait until later, you'll see. Dave will come home, reach into the drawer where I just found this, and remove the exact same one for a snack."

"Wow."

"You can say that again. And this?" he said, looking at the fruit, "...this is just the beginning of what you can do."

"It is?"

"Yup! Weren't you just thinking about your family? Don't you wanna know where they're going?"

"Well, yes, but..."

"Well, let's go then! We can talk on the way."

Traveling at the Speed of Thought

Rocket ate several pieces of his orange, which had somehow been peeled for him, and headed towards the front door. He left the remains of his snack on the floor. When I looked again, the food was gone; even the peels had vanished.

Rocket pressed his nose to one of the windows facing the street. "So here's the deal. All you have to do is think of where you'd like to be, and then wish to be there. It's really that simple!"

"*Think* of where I want to be?" I asked.

"Yup."

"And wish?"

"Yup. Think and wish." Rocket said. "Here, try this. Think about standing out in the front yard by the mailbox over there."

"Just *think* about it?"

"Yup. Just sort of, *want* to be there. Wish it."

I chuckled, closed my eyes, and thought about the family mailbox. It seemed like a silly thing to do, but somehow I knew it would work. I wished my way outside, and when I opened my eyes again, sure enough, Rocket and I were standing side-by-side right next to the mailbox. The sun was bright, the smell of winter's last remaining leaves surrounded me in a damp, earthy assault, and the breeze cooled my nose as it whispered by. We were certainly outdoors.

"Wow."

"Wow's right!" Rocket said. He walked over to the post which held the mailbox aloft and marked it.

"You still do that?" I asked.

"Sure, why not? It lets anyone who happens by know I'm here."

"Like who? We're..." I paused, thinking for a polite word, but failing to find one I continued. "We're, well, we're dead. Who's going to notice it?"

Rocket snickered. "You honestly think all of those scents you picked up on before were left by the living?"

I thought about this for a moment. The idea of detecting phantom pheromones from beyond the grave was disquieting, but stranger things had been revealed to me already.

"So...we might see others? Like us?"

"You mean dead?"

I nodded.

"Well, sure, there are souls all around us! We'll get more into that later. I'll show you how to tune into them, or ignore them. Trust me; you'll want to ignore *some* of them."

The way my father said "some of them" spooked me a little, but I kept it to myself.

Rocket continued, "For now, let's try something a bit more fun. Have you ever wanted to go somewhere you've never been? Like maybe inside one of the neighbor's houses where another dog lives, or cat, or whatever?"

I thought about that for a moment. "Someplace I've never been?"

"Yep! Someplace totally new, but keep it simple this time. I take it you have an understanding now of how big this world actually is?"

I thought about that for a moment. Until today, I'd always known the world was larger than what I'd been able to see or explore, but until that very moment when Rocket asked the question, I'd never fathomed it could be so impossibly large. That realization barreled into me with quite a bit of force, and I had to shake my head for a second.

"Just now figuring it out, huh?" Rocket asked.

I blinked my eyes and took a deep breath. "Wow, I never guessed it was so, so...." I let my voice trail off for a second as I tried to formulate my words.

"Yup, she's a big ol' ball of confusion sometimes, that's for sure," Rocket said.

"So many places, so many different *kinds* of places..."

Rocket chuckled. "That's what I was trying to say: let's just travel to an area a little closer to home this go-around."

I tried to push away the hundreds of thousands of images that had sprung to life in my head and think of a place close: somewhere I'd guessed about but had never actually seen. "Well, I've always wondered where all the food in the refrigerator comes from."

Rocket laughed, howled, and then laughed some more. "You are definitely *my* son, I'll give you that! That is the very first place I went when I started learning all of these tricks."

"Is it?"

"Yup. Nothing like dying to work up an appetite!"

I smiled. "I am a little hungry, and that orange smelled amazing back there. Like, like smiles and sunshine wrapped in a laugh."

"Now that's a description!" Rocket said. "Okay, here's the deal. Just think about the last time you remember Dave and Rebecca bringing home a bunch of food and kind of wish your way to where they got it! It's called a *grocery store* by the way."

The mailbox was one thing and simple enough; I knew exactly where it was, what it looked like, and I'd been there countless times to mark my territory. But this was something altogether different. I'd never been to the grocery store before. I had no idea where it was, and I was clueless as to what it looked like. But I gave it a go. I closed my eyes, thought of the last time my owners returned from this mysterious place, and wished myself to that exact spot. At the very last second, I wondered how Rocket would follow, but it was too late. When I opened my eyes, I was standing in the middle of a long aisle of food, surrounded by humans.

"See? Nothing to it!" Rocket said from just ahead.

"How did you follow me?"

"I just wished, or wanted, or whatever you wanna call it, to go where you went. Simple."

"Wow."

"You say that a lot, you know?" Rocket said.

"Well, give me a little credit; I've only been deceased for an hour or so."

Rocket chuckled. "You'll get the hang of it soon enough. Besides, it's not like there's a quiz at the end," he said. "Let's take a look around. Then we'll go see what your family is up to."

The store was filled with food. Everywhere I looked, food stared back at me. Vegetables, fruits, breads, you name it. There were things I'd never seen or tasted, but somehow I knew what they were. This bit is a little difficult to explain, but I'll give it a shot. For instance, I understood what *candy* was. I knew there were many different types, it was filled with sugar, and human children go quite insane over the prospect of it and lose their minds and their teeth if they eat too much of it. I wanted some immediately.

I knew that there were canned, boxed, bagged, and jarred foods—and I understood what each was. Macaroni and cheese sounded particularly interesting, and I was aware of what it would taste like once cooked and prepared. I also knew what it would smell like. I wish I could describe how wondrous *that* was. This store, this grocery store

9

was astounding. It was hard to imagine a better place to be if you could have anything you wanted, and the worst place to be if you could not.

"You gotta try chocolate," Rocket said from just ahead, and his tail began wagging at an obscene rate of speed.

"Chocolate?"

The word was familiar, I knew what it was but as far as I could remember, I'd never sampled it.

"No kidding? You've got to try some. It's amazing. One of life's cruel little tricks to us dogs if you ask me. We can't eat it when we're alive or it'll kill us, but we're all hopelessly addicted to it once we're dead. It's a vicious concoction."

"Sounds lovely."

"You have no idea," Rocket said. "I've met dogs who couldn't resist it in life and ended up here because of it. Even now, you can usually find them buried tail-deep in the stuff."

The chocolates Rocket found were called "Hershey's Kisses." They looked like little raindrops of silver that had collided with a flat surface and then frozen. They were bite-sized pieces, and each was wrapped in silver foil with a small white flag protruding from the top.

"Ignore the wrappers. I mean, just don't..." Rocket paused. "...you know... Don't *want* to taste them."

"What do you mean, don't *want* to taste them? Eat them wrappers and all?"

"Yup, just decide you don't want to taste the foil; it's kind of metallic, like drinking out of a fountain filled with change. Or you could...you could kinda do like I did with the orange back at the house, but... I'd have to explain it, and it's sort of confusing, and there's kind of a trick to it....You know what? Just eat the foil!"

I gave up trying to figure out what my now obviously energized father was talking about and stared at the silver wrapping covering each piece of candy. "And the humans cover the chocolate in this?"

"They can't taste the residue, and unwrapping each one slows them down enough so they won't eat too many... sometimes."

"Ahhh."

"Well, usually. I've been to homes where you'd swear the couch cushions were made from millions of these little, tiny, balled-up wrappers."

Rocket dragged a package from the shelf and, before I could try any, retrieved a second one and tossed it at my feet.

"You're going to eat the whole bag?" I asked.

Rocket laughed. "Ha! And then some!" He tore open the bag in one quick, almost desperate motion.

To say the chocolate was amazing would not be very accurate, or give it half the credit it deserves. Without delving into too much foreshadowing, or deterring too drastically from the story at present, I must say that in the years I've been allowed to enjoy chocolate without risk of sickness or death, I've eaten far more than you can possibly imagine. Gluttony might be a sin for the living, but for the dead, it's almost a way of life—at least where chocolate is concerned.

I will never forget that day in the grocery store with my father. We ate ourselves into a delirium, and after that, we enjoyed some more. What a perfect introduction to the afterlife it was.

"We'll take a chocolate tour one day," Rocket said. "There's a huge organization that puts one on every year. I think it starts in Mexico this time, and ends in Switzerland. I'll let 'em know we're interested."

"They have chocolate vacations?"

"Of course! You wouldn't believe the amount of dogs involved in that, oh, and bears; good grief, the bears. Now THEY can tell you a thing or two about chocolate! I'd swear they spend as much time sniffing the stuff as they do eating it. You think we can pick up on scents pretty well? We've got nothing on bears. But like I was saying, the dogs that I know involved in the chocolate tours, they spend most of the year researching new brands, factories, and concoctions. There's even a book or two on it. I'll get you one tomorrow. It explains the origins, the newest chocolatiers, and the top one hundred hot spots for the aficionados."

"A chocolate book for dogs?"

"Yup. Don't worry, you can read now, too," Rocket said, and winked his sly, know-it-all wink again.

4
Playing With Time

After we'd gorged ourselves on chocolate and sampled a few other items in the store, Rocket told me to meet him back home and he'd explain a few more things. When I arrived, I found myself lying in my old bed even though I'd imagined being in the kitchen. It was a strange, but welcome surprise. Rocket lay stretched out, eyes closed in the sunlight pouring in through the patio doors like waves of electric honey.

"So what did you think?" Rocket asked when he sensed my presence.

"I think I'll be going back to the grocery store quite often."

Rocket chuckled. "Well, while we've been off learning how to travel about and experiencing the delights of the cocoa bean, your owners have stopped at a park nearby."

"How do you know that?"

"I stopped in and checked on them halfway here."

"We were only two or three seconds apart when we left the store."

"Yeah, that reminds me. I need to fill you in on time and all that before we head off again."

"Time?"

"Yup, it's a little different now for you. It's not quite as, umm, how do I put it? It's not quite as rigid anymore. You can kinda do with it what you want."

"You're saying I can time travel? The fact I'm even acknowledging I know what that is, is…weird," I said.

Rocket grinned without opening his eyes. "Time travel? Sure. It's easy. It's a lot like the traveling we just did. All you have to do is think of a place and just add a time while you're at it, and there ya go!"

"So if I want, I can go back to when I was a puppy and see myself?"

"Sure, why not? Only there are a few rules. We haven't talked about the Man upstairs yet, but we *will* soon. He likes to stop in on everyone's first day."

"The Man upstairs? You mean God?"

"Sure, if that's what you want to call Him."

"He's going to visit?"

"I'd say the odds are good. Don't worry about it, He'll come around when He comes around, and explain a few more things. He's fun. I think you'll like him."

"Fun, huh?"

"Yup. Anyway, part of the reason *I'm* here is to teach you some things, answer some of your questions, and fill you in on the basic rules. And I'll go ahead and apologize in advance: you're going to get sick of me explaining things to you after a while, so if it gets to be too much, just let me know. I tend to ramble. Case in point."

I chuckled. "Well, right now my head is bursting with questions, so I'm happy you're here. But the rules; there are rules to being dead?"

"A bit, yeah."

"Okay, fire away."

"Well, one of the first is about bending time, or whatever you wanna call it. You *can't* talk about the future. In other words, let's say you go back and meet yourself as a puppy, like you just mentioned. You can't tell yourself anything about the future if you do. Well, not *specific* anyway. Nothing like, 'Don't run out into the road tomorrow when you escape from the backyard because a kid on a bike's going to run over you, and you'll end up in a cast for two months.' But you CAN say things like, '…it's best if you don't run out in the road anymore.' Etcetera etcetera etcetera…"

"Sounds easy enough."

"It is, and it isn't. There are times when it's downright miserable." Rocket sighed and rolled over so the sunlight could warm his belly. "Like when you KNOW something bad is going to happen. And there you are, back before whatever happened actually happens, and you can't warn anyone. Well, not really. It's complicated, but it will make sense. You'll know what you can and can't say. I'm just supposed to give you a brief lesson on it. There's a lot more to learn where time is concerned, but we'll go over it gradually. You'll find you already know a lot of these things anyway."

"What happens if I break the rules?"

"You can't," Rocked replied.

"No?"

"Nope. You might try, but you can't really break 'em. Why would you want to anyway?"

"I dunno, just curious."

13

"Yeah. I asked the same thing," Rocked said and chuckled for a moment. "Break the rules... You're definitely my boy... Your mother! That reminds me! You two have never really met! I mean, not met, met."

I was shocked. "Is she...is she still alive?"

"She sure is. She'll kill me if I don't take you to see her soon. But let's go check in on Dave, Rebecca, and Chanook first."

The news that my mother was still alive stunned me. I had a very vague memory of her, as I was only a few weeks old when we were separated. I remember being sad, and I had a hard time sleeping for a bit.

"And we can go...we can go see her? And she'll be able to see us?" I asked.

"Yup. If you *want* her to see you, that is."

"Well, I do, but...it's been a long time and... I don't really remember her."

"That's okay, she remembers *you*. I'll tell you what, we'll go check in on everyone else, and if you're feeling up to it after that, we'll go say hello to your mother."

"I don't... I don't even know her name."

Rocket stood up and walked over to where I lay. "It's Belle. But listen kid, seriously—don't worry, she'll be glad to see you! First things first, though. Let's try a little time travel, okay? We won't do too much, nothing crazy, just a slight bend or two."

I stood up and shook off the blanket of nerves that had fallen over me. I was still a bit leery about the prospect of meeting my mother, but I was able to shed my fears far more easily than I'd ever been able to before. I wasn't sure why I was anxious to meet my mother, but it seemed safe to assume I was worried about disappointing her. Why that was on my mind, I had no idea. I guess you always want to impress your mother, even if you never really knew her. But like I mentioned before, one second I was worried, and quite literally the next I felt fine.

"So let's try something easy," Rocket said. "Let's go to where your family was just after I arrived."

"You mean when I first saw you today?"

"Yup. You want to imagine traveling to see them at that particular moment in time. Think you can manage that?"

I nodded.

"Okay then, just think about your family; think about where you were when they left, and what you were doing, and just like before, just *wish* you were with them."

I closed my eyes again and tried to imagine Dave and Rebecca in the truck with Chanook. I thought about the few minutes after Rocket had arrived, and I wished. There was a brief sensation of flying, a small feeling that I'd landed on a bed of feathers, and then a sound of music filled my ears.

"Wow, you're getting good at this," Rocket said before I'd opened my eyes.

Sure enough, when I looked around, I was in the back of the family truck. There stood Chanook, panting for all he was worth and wagging his tail. Dave and Rebecca sat up front, and Rocket stood in the seats between us all.

"Looks like we've just left the neighborhood. Good work! That's a good hour or so ago," Rocket said, and continued to stare out the window.

"Wow!"

Rocket smiled. "You know what else is really neat? You'd think that you and I would be back at your home meeting again, right? Well, that's one of the beauties of the kind of time traveling we do! We're simply here now at this point in time, and not there. So that whole 'going back in time and meeting yourself' bit doesn't really apply! Well, not post-life, anyway."

I was a bit confused, so I just nodded.

"I know, I know, it can scramble your noodle if you think too much about it, but you gotta admit, it's pretty cool!"

I laughed. "I'll take your word for it."

The Living, The Dead, And The Man Upstairs

I once heard that a good soul never experiences sorrow or regret once it has left the earth; that when you die, you leave behind all of your pain and suffering, both physical and mental. Every question you've ever wanted answered, is, sadness in all its forms vanishes forever, and life, as it were, is full of joy. I can tell you that most of that is true. *Most.* And perhaps all of it is true for some. But when I arrived in the back of my family's car that day, Rocket in the seat and Chanook staring out of the windows, I was overcome with sorrow.

Let me explain. I was glad to see them again, of that there is no doubt. I was utterly elated, in fact. But things were different now, far different. Dave would no longer brush my hair and groom me as I slept. Rebecca would never scratch my head, or throw my favorite ball again. And as far as I knew, they would not see me again for many, many years to come. At least I hoped not! That day was a sad one for me in some respects. I felt as my family did, I suspect. I mourned the loss of them as they mourned losing me.

"Don't forget that you can still talk to them… *sort of,*" Rocket said.

I looked over and noticed he was staring at me.

"Don't get all down in the dumps on me yet," he said, and winked. "Why do they say that, anyway? *'Down in the dumps.'* I always thought that was a funny expression. I've had more fun in dump yards than just about anywhere else… minus the chocolate factories of course."

I laughed despite my sudden change in mood. "I wish I had known you longer."

"Me too, kiddo, me too. But hey! We've got longer than you can possibly imagine to get to know each other now!"

I forced a slight smile and looked over at Chanook. "So I can show myself to him, but not to Dave and Rebecca?"

"Well…. It's a little more complicated than that. Here's the short version. You've seen spirits all your life, but you've only known that some of them were in fact, well, spirits! I'd say ghost, but I don't like that term. Besides, there's a difference between spirits and ghosts anyway. Where was I? Oh, it's like that for us, the ability to see those who have passed on. The rules where we're concerned, animals that is, are a little different than the rules that humans live by."

"Is there a guide book I should get?"

Rocket grinned. "If you think about it, you already know everything I'm telling you."

"I do?"

"Sure. But I'll tell you anyway. You'll see. Where was I? Oh…take Chanook here for instance. You can show yourself to him if you like. You're his family. But you have to remember, he has his own life to live now, and you are no longer part of it in the traditional sense."

"But I can't let Dave or Rebecca see me?"

"No. Unfortunately, that can only happen on *very* special occasions, and trust me, you *don't* really want those to happen anyway."

"No?"

"No, it takes something like a near-death experience, or the moment before someone dies. Then you can make yourself known to comfort them. But get this… You *can* visit them in their dreams!"

"I can?"

"Sure! We'll try it tonight if you want."

"That sounds fun."

"It is. I love doing it. You can have all kinds of adventures in human dreams. They have some of the most beautiful imaginations you'll ever encounter..which also means they scare themselves half silly sometimes, but you can help with that, too."

"Wow."

"Remind me to get you a new word when I'm at the store next time."

I chuckled. "So no showing myself to humans, and where other animals are concerned, just use my better judgment?"

"There ya go."

"Sounds easy enough."

"Sometimes. Here, why don't you say hello to Chanook? Let him know you're okay."

I thought about that for a second. If it were anything like traveling through time, or just over distances, then this should be very similar. I closed my eyes, and *wished* Chanook could see me. The response was almost instant.

"DUDE!" Chanook yelped.

I opened my eyes and smiled. "Didn't think I was gone forever, did you?"

Chanook began wagging his tail and prancing about. "I was wondering! Geesh, you scared me though."

"Sorry about that."

"You look awesome! Totally glossed up and what not!" Chanook said.

"Glossed up, huh?"

"Yeah! So what's it like? Is it cool? You look way better than you did! Dude, your hips don't still hurt, do they? Geesh, I hope not, they were pretty painful, huh? I always worried about you going up and down the stairs! How did you get here? Can you fly?"

"Slow down, slow down," I replied. "Everything is fine, wonderful in fact. And no, my hips do not hurt anymore."

"Man, that's awesome! They were pretty bad at the end, huh?"

"Yes, but they feel perfectly fine now. Like new, you might say."

I wanted to tell him more, to tell him of the chocolates in the store, of Rocket and I soaring through time. I wanted to tell him what to expect when he passed on. I wanted to tell him everything that had happened to me that day. But somewhere, someone in the back of my mind told me what I should and what I should not say. It also told me that some things are better left unspoken, and there are good reasons for leaving certain questions unanswered. Sometimes, the best answer is no answer at all.

"Dude, I totally can't wait to die now!" Chanook said.

"Nook, don't say that. I don't ever want to hear you talk like that again."

Chanook cocked his head to the side, puzzled. "Sorry man, geesh. But you look so...so cool! You look so young and I don't know, different? Like, more than just happy different, but REALLY happy different! I can't figure out how to describe it."

"Well, the next time you want to hurry up and die, you think of Rebecca and Dave, and how they'd feel."

Chanook lowered his head. "Yeah. That was stupid."

"It wasn't stupid. Just think before you say something like that next time. And remember, life is the greatest gift you will ever receive." I had no idea where this little slice of sage wisdom came from, but somehow it seemed like the proper thing to say. Nook appeared to understand and nodded.

18

Rocket placed his paws on the back of the seat. "He doesn't know I'm here, so it's best we not mention it."

Chanook sniffed my neck and circled me again. "Dude... so, can you stay? I mean. Are you back? Like, back, back? For good?"

"We'll have to see about that. I'm not sure how all of this works just yet, but I *feel* like I can visit whenever I want."

"Dude, that is awesome!"

Rocket chuckled. "Remind me to get *him* some new words, too."

"What are you getting all crazy over, buddy?" a voice asked from the front of the car. It was Dave.

I looked in the mirror and saw his gaze pass right through me. It was a warm kind of feeling, but sad. Chanook of course had no idea what Dave was asking him, but he cocked his head to one side again, stopped his panting and looked back towards the front of the car.

"He wants to know what you're prancing about and wagging your tail about," I said.

"DUDE! You can understand him now?"

"Yes."

"That is so cool!"

"Yes, yes it is."

Rocket and I spent the next several hours with the family. The park where Dave and Rebecca took us was named Pleasant Grove, which in my opinion couldn't have been a more suitable title. I'd only been once before. After that, my hips had rendered the trip impossible. A small, fenced-in area for dogs to meet off-lead stood near the parking lot, several covered picnic areas for the humans and their children to eat had been erected close by, and the rest of the park was wooded. Several trails snaked through the trees, and the path we eventually found ourselves on led to a river about a mile from the parking lot.

When we left the woods, a small pebble-strewn beach greeted us. The water rolled by, clear and calm. The sunlight played delightful tricks on its surface and cast a dazzling array of prismatic colors back into the sky. Chanook ran about fetching a small red ball which Dave produced from his backpack. No matter what Dave tried, though, Chanook refused to go into the water. I was always the water dog, not my brother. Rocket was happy to chase along beside him but he would stop occasionally, cock his head from side to side, and stare off into the woods for a moment. Almost as if he'd seen or heard something in the distance; what or who it was, I didn't know. He did come over to me

19

once and asked if I'd heard puppies. I informed him that I hadn't, and Rocket went back to romping with Dave and Chanook. I found Rebecca sitting under a tree, watching her family, a small smile on her lips.

Remember me telling you that I could hear and understand my owner's thoughts? Well, now I tried my best to pay attention to Rebecca's. I lay down beside her, closed my eyes and listened. It wasn't long before I understood everything that came into her mind. Her thoughts were entirely on me. She recalled how little and playful I was when she first took me home. She remembered throwing countless balls with me, and taking me for endless walks. There was the time when I'd jumped off a two-story balcony in pursuit of a bird, and she found me in the flower bed below. Evidently I looked quite puzzled over the realization that dogs could not fly.

Rebecca cried a little from time to time, but was quick to wipe away any tears whenever Dave looked up from the beach. I could hear his thoughts as well. He was worried about Rebecca, upset over losing me, and conscious of how Chanook might be feeling all at the same time. He was complex, but guarded and quiet where his emotions were concerned. It wasn't until then that I realized how immense his heart actually was and how long and hard he'd practiced fortifying it. Why he'd done this to himself was a mystery to me.

I focused back on Rebecca. "It's okay," I whispered, and laid my head on her lap. "I'm fine." Much to my surprise, she smiled.

"Well, you seem to be getting the hang of this, all right," a new voice said from the beach.

When I looked up, I saw a tall man dressed mostly in white walking towards me. He held a small rock in one hand and was busy turning it over and over again as he approached.

"Hello?" I asked.

"Well, hello to you, Tucker!" the man replied. He looked back at the rock in his hand, turned around, and skipped it all the way across the water. He laughed, turned back to me and smiled. "I've always loved doing that."

6
A Soul Knows

"Have we met before?" I asked.

The man stepped into the shade of the tree, smiling down at Rebecca. "Oh yes. A long time ago actually, but you were just a puppy."

I can't explain how I understood who He was, or how I felt that day when we met on the beach. It's difficult to put into words, but imagine your closest friend, someone who means more to you than anyone else in the world. Now imagine living almost your entire life without being able to see them, without being able to talk to them the way you *used* to. Now imagine one day, quite unexpectedly, there they are. Try to envision knowing you'd never be apart again, and that for as long as time decides to continue ticking away, you'll always be able to see one another, whenever you want, and as often as you desire.

I stood up, leaving Rebecca to her thoughts. "Rocket said I might see you today."

"I try to greet everyone on their first day."

"Everyone?"

"Sure! Remember Rocket telling you about traveling with your mind and manipulating time, those sorts of things? Who do you think wrote the book on all of that?" the man said. "Not to mention, I have a few other tricks up my sleeves, and books, come to think of it – entire volumes actually! I have very long sleeves or many, many arms, apparently." He finished, and began to chuckle.

"Well, it's a pleasure to meet You! Umm, again?"

"The pleasure is mine, Tucker. And don't you worry about Dave and Rebecca. They will be just fine. I promise."

I relaxed a bit at that. "Thank you. I…I'm not sure what to call You? I mean… Your name?"

"Oh, I have many names. You wouldn't believe how many. I'm not certain I have a favorite, as they are almost all very good ones. What would you like to call Me?"

"I…well, I don't know? What would You like me to call You?"

"Anything you want! Pick something. I'll try it on for size."

Now imagine this. What would you do? Standing in front of you is God, and God would like you to give Him a name. Have you ever named anyone? If you've ever agonized over what to call your new baby or a pet, then you can *almost* picture my predicament. I say almost, because honestly unless you've been face to face with the Creator of all things, and He's asking you to give Him a name…well, let's just say it's a difficult task at best.

"I've always liked James?" I said.

"James? That's a good name; I've always liked it, too. Well, Tucker, call me James."

James then walked over to Rebecca. He smiled, placed a hand on her shoulder and whispered something into her ear. To this day I do not know what was said, but Rebecca's thoughts became peaceful and far more positive in an instant.

A moment later, James looked back out at the river. He watched the rest of my family for several minutes and then looked back to me. "How about a walk down the beach? We can catch up on a few things."

"That sounds nice."

James nodded, and we started down the river past Dave, Chanook and Rocket. None of them seemed to notice us.

"They'll be here when we get back. Actually, you can come back before we left a second ago," James said.

"I will, I mean I can? Oh right, the whole time thing."

James smiled. "You have to enjoy going where you want and *when* you want to go."

"It is pretty nice."

"So how is your first day going so far?" James asked. "Do you have any questions for me?"

"I'm sure I do, I just can't think of them at the moment. Give me a few minutes; I'm sure I'll bombard you!"

James laughed, and the sound of it warmed me.

"Rocket's been a big help," I said.

James nodded. "Rocket's a good dog. I've always enjoyed his sense of humor."

We walked along and I thought about what questions to ask, and how to ask them. I was a little nervous, and I didn't want to ask just any question and certainly didn't want to sound foolish.

"You are not going to sound foolish, Tucker," James said.

"Thank you."

James nodded. "Rocket mentioned going to see your mother soon, didn't he?"

"Actually, he did. Belle. I'm a little nervous about it."

"Well, why don't we go together?"

22

"Really? You, You wouldn't mind?"

"Of course not."

Before I could say thank you, I found myself standing in a large building surrounded by other dogs.

"Oops, I should have probably warned you," James said. "We're in North Carolina now. Belle has lived here for the last nine years. Her owner's names are Melissa and Ryan Gentry; I like them very much. They have several dozen acres of land and raise horses that they use to rehabilitate young children with disabilities or injuries. It's a noble pursuit."

"Wow," I said, and took in my surroundings.

It became apparent after a moment or two that we were inside a rather large barn. I'd been inside one or two in my time, as Rebecca was very fond of horses and took me to see them when she could. To either side of us, light-colored wooden stalls lined the walls. Some of them were closed, while a handful stood ajar. On most of the stall doors, brass plates had been fastened which were adorned with various names. There was Handsome, Clover, Daisy, Midnight, and more. The dogs that roamed the barn sniffed about and seemed quite at home.

James motioned to a few of the dogs. "Most of these young fellows are your brothers, believe it or not."

"They are?"

"Oh yes. You have fourteen brothers, and an even larger number of nephews."

"No sisters or nieces?"

"No, unfortunately. But in all, you have thirty-seven relatives still living."

"Wow."

"Rocket was right about your favorite word."

I chuckled, and James winked down at me.

"Shall we go and see Belle?" He asked.

"Yes, please."

We walked the length of the barn to the last stall on the left. The hay inside smelled fresh, and a large fleece-covered bed rested in one corner. On this bed lay my mother. She looked tired but awake. Her hair was a smooth caramel with flecks of silver running here and there. Her eyes were vivid brown, and her paws were almost all white. She lay with her head facing the door, watching the entrance to the barn and the activities beyond.

"Can she see us?" I asked.

"No, not yet. Not unless you want her to."

I thought about that for a minute as I looked at Belle. My nerves calmed and I began to notice something, a misty image behind her eyes. She was thinking about her family and how she would miss them.

"What does she mean?" I asked without offering an explanation.

"Today's her last day here, Tucker."

"You mean she's dying?"

"Yes."

It was then that I understood why James offered to accompany me.

"Does Rocket know?"

"No, not yet. That's why I decided maybe it was best if I came along. Is that okay?"

I swallowed the lump which had climbed into my throat. "Yes, thank you."

James put a hand on my head. "Don't be sad, Tucker. Belle's had a long and wonderful life. I am very proud of her, and so you should be."

"It's strange that we would both die on the same day."

"You were her firstborn," James said. "And sometimes...sometimes, mothers know."

I didn't ask what he meant. I didn't need to. I understood that sometimes in life, a soul knows when certain events transpire and when to let go of this world in response. It just made sense.

"Is she in pain?"

"No, she's just very tired."

"Should I...I mean...should I let her see me?"

"Do you want to?"

"I think I do."

Belle looked up from her bed and smiled. "I was wondering if you would stop by today."

7

Angels

I was a bit taken aback when Belle looked at me. I knew that I wanted her to see me, to know I was with her, but there still lingered a nervous bit of indecision rolling about in my brain when she did. Have you ever been with someone who just happened to know what you wanted at a particular moment in time? Someone who seemed to know exactly what your wish was, even before you did? When I think back to Belle that day, and her sudden ability to see me, that's what I am reminded of, someone who knows you better than you know yourself, even if only for an instant. That is a rare gift in life, and I pity those who never experience it.

I was overwhelmed when Belle spoke to me, as you can imagine. But I was astonished to discover that she recognized me. She wagged her tail in soft pleasant arcs and smiled the kind of smile only mothers possess: the kind that can wash away all of your fears, all of your sorrows, and all of your concerns. Almost all mothers know a kind of magic, and you can see it when they smile at their children.

"You know…" I started and had to clear my throat, "You know me?"

"Of course I do, Pickle."

"Pickle?"

"Well, that's what you were called when you were here with me. I kind of liked it. What's your name now?"

"Tucker."

"Tucker, you say? I like it, it suits you. A little more sturdy then Pickle, but not nearly as cute," Belle said. We both smiled.

James walked over to the barn's two large doors and looked out over the pasture beyond. "I'll be back in a while, Tucker. You two take all the time you like."

I looked back to James and nodded. I knew I shouldn't mention him to Belle just yet.

"Is it okay if I lay here with you for a while?" I asked.

Belle laughed a small, tired laugh and nodded. "You don't need to ask me those kinds of questions, Pickle, sorry, Tucker. You know you can lie down next to me if you like."

I walked over and circled about in the hay for a moment. As I did, Belle licked my cheek and beamed. It seemed natural that she could do so. Not even death can stop a mother's tender affection.

"So today was your time, was it?" Belle asked.

"I guess so," I said. "But how did you know it was today?"

"I'm not really sure, to be honest," Belle replied. "I just knew somewhere in my heart that you would be seeing me today. At least I guessed you would."

I nodded. "I have to admit that today has been strange, but brilliantly strange!"

"You weren't in any pain, were you?" Belle asked.

"Well, not at the end."

"What was it, then? Your hips?"

"How did you know that?"

"You smiled a little when you lay down next to me, as if you hadn't been able to do that in a long time, not easily, anyway."

"You know, I could have been smiling because I was lying down next to you for the first time since I was a pup."

"No, that was the smile you had after I kissed you."

I felt my cheeks flush and my eyes begin to tear. "Well, you must have been right, then. It is nice not to be in pain each time I stand or sit or lay down. Actually, it's nice not to be in pain each time I do anything!"

Bell chuckled. "It's always the hips. Your grandfather had the same problem. So did his father and so on and so on. At least that's what I was told. I'd hoped it would skip you."

"It didn't really get bad until the very end, so I guess it could have been much worse."

Belle nodded. "Well, I'm glad you're here, and I'm sorry at the same time, Tucker."

"Me, too."

We talked for what seemed hours. Belle told me of her family here and her adventures on the farm. She pointed out my oldest brother and several of his sons. We spoke of my family at length. Belle laughed several times over Chanook and some of the tales I told her of him. When the sun faded behind the trees, several of my brothers and nephews gathered around, and Belle slipped into dreams.

We lay near her for quite some time. I chose not to show myself to the others, but I did listen to their thoughts and comforted them when

26

I felt I should. One of the younger dogs, Wicket, was very upset over Belle's health. I walked over to him occasionally and did what I could to put his mind at ease, but his sadness would always return despite my efforts. Perhaps I was not strong enough to help those in such need just yet, and that thought concerned me. Belle's owners came to the barn several times and sat with us until retiring for the night. Soon everyone was asleep, and the lights over the stalls were turned off, save Belle's.

"Tucker?" a voice said from the barn's doorway.

I looked up to see James and Rocket. "I think it's time," I told them.

"It is," James replied. "Would you come with us, please?"

James and Rocket turned and walked out into the night. I followed as asked. We climbed a large hill overlooking the farm and a wide, bluish-green river. The night air was cool, clear, and full of wonderful smells. Millions of stars glimmered above, and a soft silver moon lit the hillside. We stood there for a while in silence. I thought of Belle and the others in the barn below. Even the horses outside of their paddocks had come through to see her once or twice. They knew as well as the others that she would no longer be with them in the morning. That was the first time I had seen a horse since my new life and though I did not consciously wish for them to see me in return, each one seemed to do just that as they walked by, as if we all understood the same secret. Horses are magnificent creatures.

After a while, James looked back down to the barn and smiled. I followed his gaze towards a small path leading to where we now stood. A lone figure walked towards us in the moonlight.

8
<u>Family</u>

When was the last time you saw someone and thought that they were perfect? Think back and try to remember someone who seemed utterly flawless to you. For some, that feeling comes when they see their newborn child for the first time. For others, it's seeing a true love.

I can tell you it's the same for animals as it is for humans. Every now and then that special soul appears in your life and no matter how others may perceive them, regardless of how they see themselves, to *you* they are perfect. I've experienced that feeling several times. The first was when I met James on the riverside that sunny day in May. The second was when I saw my mother walking across the farm later that same night. If you haven't encountered a soul like this yet in your life, trust me, you will. And once it happens, the time it took for you to meet them will seem trivial and well worth the wait.

"I...I should have brought something..." Rocket whispered.

"You did, you brought yourself," James said, and patted Rocket on the head. "I can't think of a better gift."

"I'll bet she would enjoy that chocolate tour you were telling me about," I offered.

Belle came over the rise and smiled at the three of us as she approached. Her fur shined bright in the moonlight, and her eyes shimmered. She looked far younger and far more radiant than I could have ever imagined. A warm breeze carried the scent of young May flowers up from the river below, as if to welcome my mother to her new life.

James smiled. "Hello, Belle."

"Hello," Belle replied. "I seem to...I mean...I feel like we've met?"

James laughed. "You would be surprised how often I get that. Point in fact we have, but you were very, very young."

Belle studied James for a moment. "Sometimes...I mean, I think...sometimes, I have dreams of you...of...before I was born. And we used to play? Were those real? I mean, are those memories?"

James clapped his hands. "Some of them are, yes! I'm glad you remember. We had a lot of fun, you and me."

"Hello, Belle," Rocket said. He stared at the ground for a moment and seemed unsure of what to do or say next.

"Rocket? You old scoundrel, you! How have you been?" Belle asked, and began laughing.

"Good, good...I've been showing our son here the ropes all day."

"Rocket has been helping me for years, actually," James said. "He's quite a good teacher, if you ask me."

Belle looked up at James and then back to Rocket. "Years?"

Rocket looked embarrassed. "Umm...well...yeah...."

"Don't tell me it was a car."

Rocket did not reply, but he did nod a little.

"At least it was a '68 Stingray. There are worse ways to go," James said, and winked at my father.

The four of us talked well into the night. Belle asked many of the same questions I had and seemed just as mesmerized by her new life. James said he especially liked to see all mothers on their first day, to say hello and to thank them. It was hard to imagine the intricacies involved in that sort of effort, and I puzzled over it for weeks afterwards. Just before dawn, James offered to take Belle to see Wicket, as he was undoubtedly having a very hard time saying goodbye to her. James also mentioned Belle's mother and some sort of mysterious celebration he needed to get her to before long. Aside from the celebration being a secret, James would say no more, but he did promise we would all have a grand time. Everyone agreed to meet again shortly, and Rocket made a point of promising chocolate all around.

My father and I stood on the hilltop watching James and Belle make their way to the barn.

"Are you ready to go back to the river, then?" my father asked. "When I left, Chanook was actually attempting the water."

"He was?"

"Yep. I dunno what got into him, but he was trying it out. Maybe he realized life's too short not to at least *try* a thing."

"That sounds fun," I replied. I was still a little numb from seeing my mother and a bit overwhelmed with the day's events. I think Rocket sensed it before we left.

"When we get there, I was wondering if you could help me with something?"

"Sure. What is it?"

"Well, there's a little boy out there, and from what I understand, he's been there for a very long time."

"A boy? What do you mean?"

"I mean I think he died there a while ago. From what I gathered, he's pretty much avoided everyone who's come to help. Even you-know-who.... I don't know why, but in situations like this sometimes dogs like us can help, and...."

I interrupted. "You're telling me there's a ghost of a little boy out by the river, and he's been avoiding everyone?"

"Yep. James said the boy's name is Colin, and he's been waiting for me."

"What does that mean?"

"I have absolutely no idea! Figured we'd go check it out."

And so we were off, back to the river, back to my family, and back to a little boy who had died there many years before.

9
<u>Colin</u>

When we returned to Pleasant Grove, it was early afternoon. I found myself quite literally *where* and *when* I had departed with James. Rebecca was still sitting under the tree, while Dave and Chanook played near the water. By all rights I SHOULD have been looking back at myself.

"I need to get used to this time travel thing," I said.

"Yep, it's a bit weird at first, especially when one day seems to last an entire week or more. It can be a little confusing."

"I don't feel tired, though."

"Well, I'd hope not!" Rocket said. "You don't have that old body that needs rest anymore! But don't worry; you can still take naps whenever you want. What would the afterlife be like if you couldn't snooze from time to time?"

"So I can sleep even though I'll never get tired?"

"Yep! Like eating, even though you'll never get hungry."

I marveled at this, and we walked over to where Dave and Chanook amused one another in the shallows. I decided not to show myself to my brother just yet. There was still the issue of Colin, and I wasn't entirely sure how that was going to play out. Rocket walked down the river to see if he could find the boy, and I sat and watched the water and my family.

For a time I tried to imagine why a little boy would hide here after he'd passed on. I thought of James, and how He had come to me. I had immediately trusted Him, and would have gone wherever He chose. I had, in fact. So why this little boy would feel threatened or try and hide from James, or anyone for that matter, was bewildering.

Shortly after I passed on, Rocket appeared. When Belle died, some of her family was there to greet her. Even if the boy's parents were still alive, it made sense that some of his relatives would have come to say hello, or to take him in. It even seemed safe to assume that Colin might have understood how to see his parents, or his family. I understood a great many things inexplicitly, so why wouldn't he? And if Colin had, why would he choose to stay here? I also agonized over how, if at all, I could help the boy. What if I did more harm than good? What if I frightened him? I hadn't even been able to help poor little Wicket.

31

Rocket interrupted my thoughts. "I think I found him," he said as he trudged through the tall grass beside me. It was strange to see him wade through the reeds and flowers and not disturb any of them.

"Where is he? Did he talk to you?" I asked.

"He's on the bank, just around the bend a ways. And no, I kept my distance. I think he knew I was there, though. I mean, it makes sense that he would."

"Well, what do we do?"

"I think we should both go and try to talk to him. See if he needs help, or try and figure out why he's been hiding here for so long."

I nodded and stood to follow Rocket. As we left, I glanced back towards my family and put myself in Colin's place. What would I do if I ever lost them entirely? The prospect was frightening, terrifying even.

We found Colin on the edge of the river. He looked much younger than I'd imagined. His hair was blonde and straight. He wore small tan overalls with a red and white striped shirt. His shoes were blue-green, as were his eyes. He tossed small pebbles into the water and hummed a little tune as we approached. We slowed our steps, and I wondered if someone still alive should happen to walk around the bend, would they see tiny rocks hurling themselves off into the water, or just tiny splashes which they would assume were fish or would they see nothing at all? As we grew closer, Colin turned towards us and froze.

"Hello!" Rocket said when it looked as if Colin might run or hide.

The boy did not respond.

Rocket muttered something and then cleared his throat. "Have you seen any puppies run through here, by chance?"

Colin looked surprised at the question and furrowed his brow. I have to admit I was surprised as well.

"I think he was just imagining puppies....Got me, I just saw a flash from him," a voice whispered in my head. It was Rocket's.

"Puppies?" Colin asked after a moment.

Rocket nodded. "Yep, I was just curious if any had run by here recently."

Colin glanced to me and then back to Rocket. "I don't... I mean I haven't seen any puppies," he replied. "Did you lose some?"

Rocket laughed. "Oh no, no, no... I was just curious. They just seemed to pop into my head all of a sudden; I have no idea why!"

Colin continued to stare at Rocket, but said nothing.

32

"Maybe it's the weather," Rocket said.

A question fell over Colin's face.

"You know, perfect day for puppies to be out and about and all that," Rocket said.

Colin's lips began to form a slight smile, but quickly returned to their original state. "Yeah...." he said in a small voice.

"Well, we'll be off then...."

Colin continued to stare at Rocket and I. He seemed on the verge of saying something, but stared back down at the rock in his hand and then out at the water.

"You have a good day!" Rocket added and turned around. This was not the approach I was thinking of, I'll be honest.

"Work with me here, I'm making this up as I go along." Rocket's voice echoed in my thoughts again.

Rocket speaking only in my mind was surprising as you can imagine. Having someone else's voice in your head, an intelligent interactive voice... it's bizarre. I made a mental note to ask Rocket how he spoke to me in that manner, and then disregarded the notion as it seemed to make sudden and obvious sense. You just *did*, and that was that.

I took a chance and turned back to Colin. "Unless you might want to come with us?"

Rocket turned around to face the boy again. "That sounds fun. Are you here with anyone? I mean, do you need to be anywhere anytime soon? We only saw *our* family back there on the beach, no one else."

Colin turned his gaze back to the water and stared. "No, I'm by myself," he said, and looked long and hard at the river.

I tried as best I could to read Colin's thoughts, to understand him, but for some reason I was unable to hear a single thing within the boy's mind.

"I can't really read him either," Rocket whispered in my own thoughts. *"All I got was the puppy thing."*

"Well, do you have any family nearby, or a home?" Rocket asked.

Colin remained silent, but he remained, so that was a good sign.

"You know, my brother is just down the beach trying to figure out how to swim for the first time!" I offered. "Maybe you'd like to meet him? Well, meet him in a way, I guess; he can't really see us unless we want him to, as you know."

33

Colin looked back at me. "Your brother?"

"Well, we grew up together. We share different mothers, but I've always thought of him as my brother. His name is Chanook. Would you like to meet him? I mean, he's not a puppy, but he certainly acts like one."

Colin seemed to consider this for a moment. Rocket and I remained silent, afraid the boy would vanish. After a time, Colin dropped the rock he was holding and walked towards us.

"He's here? Close by?" Colin asked.

"Yes, he's just around the corner," I replied. "If you listen, you can hear him splashing about."

Colin stopped for a moment and did just that. A soft splash of water and a tiny trickle of laughter floated up into the air from festivities unseen.

Rocket began to chuckle. "He fell in the water a few minutes ago; you should have seen him."

Colin's tiny smile tried to reappear but faded again. "Okay."

"What do we do when we get him there? I mean, what do we say?" I asked Rocket with my mind.

"I have no idea, kiddo. No idea at all."

10
<u>Lost Soul</u>

Have you ever known something to be true, a fact that is completely and utterly undeniable? Yet with all of your heart, with all of your soul, with all of your being, you refused to accept it? Discovering a loved one has deceived you, or perhaps the unexpected death of a close friend or family member? These seem like appropriate analogies. Undeniable facts, but somehow, for some reason and for some amount of time, you refuse to acknowledge it?

Now, think about what you would do if you suddenly found your life cut short. Everything you'd ever dreamed of doing in your time, all of the places you wanted to see, all the things you wanted to accomplish were instantly stripped away without warning. Now, imagine that happening to a child.

When we found Colin, Rocket and I were faced with exactly that: a young boy whose life had been lost when it had barely begun. To say I was saddened by this knowledge would not do justice to my feelings for the boy. I could sense the same sentiments from Rocket as we walked down the riverbank. Colin followed us from a distance and always seemed on the verge of dashing off into the trees and shadows beyond. Yet something kept him with us, curiosity perhaps.

When we reached the spot where my family had set up camp, everyone stopped. Colin peered out across the beach and watched as Dave threw a tennis ball several feet into the water. Chanook bounced left and right as the ball slowly floated downstream and barked crazily as if to work up his own nerves to retrieve the ball, either that or convince the ball to come to him through sheer intimidation. Dave encouraged Chanook as best he could and even stepped out into the water a bit in an effort to coax him in.

Rocket laughed. "He sure doesn't like the water, does he?"

"He never has. I honestly can't explain it," I replied.

Colin cleared his throat and looked past Dave and Chanook to a small island in the middle of the river. He stared for a while and ran his fingers over the side of his head.

"Do you like to swim?" Rocket asked the boy.

Colin looked back to us and then back out at the water. He immediately dropped his hand from his temple. "Not anymore."

A loud splash distracted us, and we all looked to see Chanook neck deep in the river, paddling as best he could after the escaping tennis ball. Dave laughed and cheered him on from the beach.

"About time!" Rocket said. "Come on, let's go a little closer."

"I have to go," Colin said, and spun around.

"You okay?" Rocket asked.

Colin stopped and glanced back over his shoulder. "I don't like it here,"

Before Rocket or I could respond, Colin vanished.

My father sighed and dropped his head. "I was afraid of that."

"Afraid of what?"

"I was afraid he'd do exactly what he did. Pop off like that. He's lost."

"He didn't seem lost."

"No, I mean he's a lost soul. It happens sometimes."

"What does that mean exactly?"

"Colin's not ready to accept the fact he's no longer alive. He doesn't want to move on, to start living again and until he does, there's no one, not even you-know-who, will be able to help him."

"Is that why we couldn't read his thoughts?"

"Yep. He didn't want us to know what he was thinking, so he shut us out. The puppy thing must have just been luck."

"So what do we do? How do we help him?"

"I'm not really sure, to be honest."

"What did James say? Let's go find Him! He'll know what to do!"

Rocket smiled. "He *does* know what to do, and he's already done it. He sent *us* here."

"Yes, but…."

"You know the phrase 'God works in mysterious ways'?"

"I think so, yes."

"Well, this is one of those times. We can't expect to know everything, even now when it seems we understand just about anything we want, whenever we want to comprehend it; case in point, that very phrase."

I didn't like Rocket's answer, but to be fair, it did make some sense to me. Why would James force a child like Colin to accept something he wasn't ready to? Why would He force anyone to do anything for that matter? Maybe the best James could do was help in

Colin's case. I wasn't certain Rocket and I were the best candidates for the job, especially me, but who was I to argue?

"So, what now?" I asked.

Rocket thought for a moment. "I think I have an idea. Let's go see his parents. And remind me to keep thinking of puppies. There has to be something in that. I have no idea what, but there has to be something to it."

"Colin's parents? What will that do?"

"I have no clue, kiddo. But we've got to start somewhere, right?"

I looked back to my family and then down the river where we had found Colin. "I guess you're right."

"Oh, I'm not sure it's the right thing to do, I just don't know where else to begin," Rocket said.

I was desperate to help the boy. "It's better than doing nothing."

"So you know where we're going?" Rocket asked.

I nodded. "I think I do. I just *want* to be with Colin's parents, right?"

"Now you're getting the hang of this," Rocket said.

"How do we know they're together, though? I mean right at this moment? If I think of being with both of them, what happens if they're, I don't know, separated, or…."

"What does your gut tell you?"

"What do you mean?"

"I mean, you were just wondering if they were both in the same place, and then you started wondering if they were even still alive."

"Well, yes."

"So what's your gut instinct? What is your heart telling your soul?"

I had to think about that for a minute. I pictured Colin in my mind, and then I tried to envision his parents. Sure enough, a brilliant and clear image of them ignited in my thoughts.

"They live near the ocean now. In a small yellow house with light blue storm shutters. There's a tiny rose garden in the back yard and a dogwood tree in the front."

"See how easy that was?"

I nodded. "I'm still getting used to knowing all of these…these *things*…. Hearing a person's thoughts, or understanding a thing simply because I *want* to… it's a little overwhelming."

Rocket winked. "It gets easier."

The Lost And The Pound

When I opened my eyes, the sunlight burned into them. As I blinked away several tears, I noticed we were standing on a small sand dune facing the ocean. And then I thought how odd it was that I should be blinking away tears at all. I guessed even the dead are still in need of a good cry from time to time.

The ocean was alive and agitated; large and small whitecaps alike dotted its face, as if excited or anxious for some reason. A sturdy wind rushed across the water and over the beach, whipping salt and sand into the air. Occasionally you could taste the ocean in the breeze. The smell was fantastic. Several people rested in lawn chairs, some walked about, and at least three or four dogs ran back and forth along the waterline, their owners tossing balls or toys from a distance.

"It's been a while since I've been here," I said.

"Me, too," Rocket replied. "It always reminds me of home, especially the smell. I don't know why I don't come back more often."

We walked out over the sand and took note of the various humans and animals that had come to the beach that afternoon.

"Which ones do you *think* they are?" Rocket asked before I could.

"I was just about to...."

Rocket chuckled. "I know. Look at the different people milling about, or sitting in their chairs, and ask yourself, which ones belong to Colin?"

I glanced from one person to the next and finally settled on a very quiet couple sitting side by side in two white and yellow chairs. I closed my eyes for a moment and tried to listen to their thoughts. First the sounds of the waves tumbling onto the beach faded, then the rushing noise of wind melted away, and finally everything else. These were Colin's parents; there was no question about it. Both had very clear, extremely focused images of the boy within their minds.

"Can you hear them? Do you think you can understand them? Understand their stories? Their lives?" Rocket's voice asked within my thoughts.

"I think so."

"Try then. Try to know them."

I focused on Colin's mother. Her name was Evelyn, though everyone called her Evie or just plain E. She was thirty-three years old, and she was pregnant for the second time in her life. Her husband's name was Eric, and he, too, was sometimes called E by their friends. Quite often they were referred to as *"The E's,"* as in *"The E's are coming over..."* or *"The E's are late again..."* or *"Everyone, these are the E's, the E's, this is everyone."* Evelyn's sister always called her Ebert, though, and as far as I could tell, she was the only one that did so.

Colin occupied both Evelyn's and Eric's thoughts. The two had just discovered that a new baby was forecast in their immediate future, and the emotions surrounding this news were as varied as emotions *could* be. Eric was shocked at first, then elated, and now he wrestled with pangs of guilt and remorse. Evelyn was afraid, excited, and angry all at the same time. She feared losing another child; she blamed herself for Colin's death, and she worried her husband did as well. A new baby should be an exciting time for those involved; at least that's what she had been raised to believe. This, *this* was not how she wanted to react to the news of a new life.

What kind of parent had she been to Colin? What kind of mother takes her eight-year-old son to the river, only to let him drown when she wasn't looking? What gave her the right to have another child when her first had died so senselessly? Regardless of how hard she tried, Evelyn couldn't even remember the name of the book she had been reading when Colin slipped and fell unconscious into the water. Was the book so unremarkably horrid that she could not recall what it was? Or was she so irresponsible that a mediocre piece of literature could captivate her so fully, so thoroughly that she would allow her only child to drown just yards away? Or was the book so well written, so miraculously conceived that even Colin's last breaths would have to wait until the end of a particularly engrossing chapter? She had not read another novel in the three years since.

I tore my mind from Evelyn's and looked to Rocket. He was shaking his head and muttering to himself.

"I guess you don't have to die to be a lost soul," I said.

Rocket looked up and sighed. "No. No, you do not."

I tried to limit Evelyn's thoughts from entering my own for a while after that. If you've ever been close someone whose heart is broken, you'll understand. Sometimes, it doesn't matter what type of mood you're in, or how wonderful you feel; there are times when another soul's emotions can seep into you and shape your own. Evelyn's emotions were some of the most powerful I had ever experienced, and it took a great deal of concentrated effort on my part to shed their effects. I couldn't help Colin if I was absorbed in his parents' anguish.

I learned a bit more about the two when I could. Eric knew his wife was afraid that he blamed her for their son's death. In fact, he held her no more responsible than he did the moss on which Colin had slipped. He too had been at the river that day and nothing, not even his own past experience saving lives in the Coast Guard, could have helped their son. It was no one's fault. Colin had waded out to that very spot countless times before at Pleasant Grove, and no amount of blame could erase the fact that sometimes, accidents happen; good or bad, they just happen.

Eric and Evelyn moved back to their hometown after Colin's death. They had family there and more importantly, there were fewer reminders of the son they had lost. Sometimes, the only way to heal a broken heart is to try and forget a little bit of what broke it in the first place, even if that something meant the world to you, or *was* the world to you. The simple act of not driving by Pleasant Grove on the way to work, or catching sight of the swing set Eric had built for Colin in the backyard, or even seeing the elementary school busses cruise by the home in the afternoon, helped to some degree.

Colin had been buried near his home, and for the last three years, neither Eric nor Evelyn had been able to visit his grave. Eric simply couldn't, and Evelyn was incapable of going alone. It was the engravings on the headstone that were the hardest. The miniscule span of years separating Colin's date of birth and the date of his death seemed insulting. And no matter how hard each of them tried, the image of those engraved mathematical facts haunted the two. Their son had died having lived only eight years.

"We're going to need more help," Rocket said at last.

I was about to say the same thing, but was otherwise engaged in wishing that Rocket would pull some piece of prophetic guidance or advice from his proverbial hat of endless knowledge. After all, he was the certified phantom here, not I.

"No wonder James sent us! Did you catch that last bit from the husband?" Rocket asked. "About Colin's dog?"

"Colin had a dog?"

"He still does. Her name is Ginger. Eric was thinking about Colin, and then he was wondering what ever happened to 'good ol' Ginger' as he put it."

I thought about that for a moment and slowly the image of a red and white English Spaniel glimmered to life in my mind. She was a beautiful dog, but was in desperate need of grooming and a better diet. I concentrated as best I could on her, and slowly, several aspects of her surroundings began to materialize in my head. She lay in a small concrete and metal enclosure. Beneath her, a tattered blue and white bed served as a resting place, and two large metal bowls rested to the side. But beyond all of this, the most noteworthy of Ginger's surroundings were the dozen or so pink and white puppies curled up next to her.

"Eric thinks she died a couple of years ago, and Colin has no idea that Ginger was lost," Rocket said. "At least, as far as I can tell Colin doesn't know; it's still hard to read him. But he must sense the puppies. That has to be part of why we picked up on that image."

"You can detect his thoughts from here?" I asked.

"Sure, why not. Proximity has got pretty much zilch to do with reading thoughts. Time either. I only brought you here to Colin's parents to get you used to all of this. We could have read them from anywhere."

I nodded. "Well, maybe we can…I don't know, maybe we can tell Colin that Ginger is lost and we found her. Maybe he will want to help her. Maybe he actually knows she needs help, and that's why he was thinking of her puppies earlier?"

"That's what I was getting at, but…." Rocket trailed off for a second. "Did you see all of them? The puppies?"

"I think so, why?"

"A couple of them aren't going to live very long."

I sighed; there went my good news to Colin theory. And besides my own death, I'd been surrounded by loss from all sides today. My mother, Colin and now some of Ginger's pups were going to die.

"You mentioned this getting easier?"

Rocket looked over and smiled. "Don't worry, kiddo, I have an idea."

"I hope so, because frankly I don't know what to do now. What are your thoughts?"

"Well first, we need more help like I said. I'll explain on the way…oh, yeah! This will be your first time up *there*, won't it?" Rocket asked. He began wagging his tail.

"Up where?"

Rocket grinned. "Up… Up-up! Ol' Bone Yard in the Sky!"

"The ol' what?"

"That's just what I like to call it. Okay, here's how we get there, it's pretty simple…." Rocket began.

12

The Ol' Bone Yard In The Sky

Home. I can think of no better word to describe Heaven. I know I'm not the first to describe it in this manner, and I won't be the last. Certainly one day you will know exactly what I mean, and perhaps you will find a better description. If you do, by all means stop by and let me know. If you've been paying attention to this tale so far, you will know *exactly* how to find me.

Rocket's advice on how to travel to Heaven was simple. He told me to close my eyes, wish to go to the first home I'd ever had, and that was really it. For a moment I imagined I'd end up back in the house where my mother brought me into this world. When I opened my eyes, however, that could not have been further from the truth.

"Pretty, huh?" Rocket asked after several long moments. You see, I was at a loss for words.

"I…" was about all I mustered for a few minutes more.

Rocket chuckled and continued wagging his tail. "Well, follow me then. And try to pick up your jaw, it's embarrassing," he added with a wink.

I tore my eyes from the spectacles surrounding me and glanced at my father for a fraction of a second; after that, I lost myself gazing about again as we walked. Everywhere I looked there were buildings. Only these structures were like nothing I had ever seen. Some stretched off into the clouds and vanished; others were small and quaint. One seemed to be made entirely of glass, while another appeared to be made from a brilliantly polished metal with hues of soft blue, red and silver. More than one building seemed to have grown from the earth itself.

Besides the buildings, enormous trees lined the streets ahead of us. Some boasted leaves of green and others were multicolored, as if permanently adorned in their best fall attire. Several trees appeared to be made of colored glass, as they were completely transparent, trunks, branches and leaves alike. I'd never seen anything like them; my favorites were the blues and yellows.

There were people and animals everywhere, young, old and ancient. Some hurried by to destinations unknown, while others strolled along appearing to simply enjoy the splendid weather at the most casual pace they cared to muster. Beings I did not recognize glided throughout the throngs. Some appeared humanoid. Others looked more reptilian than anything else, and there were some that I could not place whatsoever.

A boisterous group of children sprinted past us towards an enormous grassy field while a wide variety of excited animals giving chase. The area they raced towards was dotted with various playthings, and in the far distance, snow-capped mountains lined the horizon.

As Rocket and I walked, I noticed that we were treading on perfectly manicured grass, our footsteps never seeming to damage a single blade. Not only that, but the grass appeared to be littered with various microscopic flowers. Some looked like miniature roses, some were orchids; there were even tiny daisies mixed throughout. The overall effect was stunning, and it gave the grass an early morning, dew-covered appearance, as if the sun was busy casting rainbow-colored prisms through crystal droplets of moisture across the landscape. There were no paved streets that I could see anywhere and so far, there had not been a single car. There would be, but this particular area was automotive-free.

The street or road or path, whatever you wanted to call it, ran lengthwise next to a single enormous building which disappeared into the clouds above. Just when I thought the structure could be no larger, the street turned, and the building exploded all the way to the horizon.

"What on earth is in there?" I asked when my voice returned.

"Nothing," Rocket replied.

"Why would you build something that large and not put anything in it?"

"Oh, it's full! It's the largest building here, in fact."

"You just said it was empty."

"No, I said nothing *on earth* is in there," Rocket said, and began to chuckle.

I sighed but smiled anyway. "Well?"

"That's the building of literature. Every book... well, ALMOST every book ever written is in there. I spent an entire summer in the west quarter a couple of years ago; day and night. You wouldn't believe how many books there are."

"So it's like a giant library?"

"Sure, only you don't need a card, and any book you want is always in stock. I'm surprised you acknowledged knowing what a library is, in fact!"

I hadn't thought of that. When Rocket said the word, it simply made perfect sense. I'd never read a book, never read a single word, in fact. Yet I instantly understood what a library was and what exactly it was used for.

"That is a bit strange," I said.

"Most animals take a while to warm to their new... understandings.... You're doing pretty well, I gotta admit!" Rocket said.

"So are humans the top? I mean... it seems like everything I know now that I didn't know before, well, it all focuses on humans. Chocolates and reading and I dunno, even James looked human."

"Are we lesser creatures?" Rocket asked.

"I guess that's what I'm getting at."

"Do you feel like a lesser creature?"

"Well, no, but... it seems like such a *human* world."

"What makes you think you're not human?"

"You know all these answers in the form of questions... it's getting a little annoying."

Rocket laughed. "Sorry. My point is: do you *want* to be human?"

"No, but..."

"Then what difference does it make?"

"I guess it doesn't."

"Exactly. A soul is a soul regardless of how small or how large, or whether or not it has four legs or two, or none at all. The world doesn't revolve around opposable thumbs, ya know!"

And again I was faced with understanding a phrase I'd never heard before and its significance to our conversation. I laughed.

"Don't worry kiddo, you've got a long time to take everything in; don't try and do it all at once."

"I guess so," I replied, and offered my father a smile.

"Besides! Now that we're here..."

Rocket was suddenly and violently interrupted by three other dogs who tackled him on the spot. I froze, half expecting a fight to ensue. Instead, the only sounds I heard from the now rolling and broiling ball of fur was laughter—gales and gales of laughter.

"Rocket! Where have you been, mate?" one of the pack asked when everyone had settled.

"Yeah! You off and disappear on us *and* you block us at the same time? You better have a good reason, ya mutt!" an impossibly large St. Bernard said.

Rocket stood up and tried to slow his pants. "Gents… this here's my boy! Name's Tucker, and I expect you to show him the same courtesy you show me!"

The three dogs all turned in my direction. There was an Australian cattle dog, the St. Bernard, and a very bulky Bulldog. No one said a word.

"Hello," I offered the trio.

There was a moment of utter silence from the pack, and then finally the cattle dog stepped forward and circled me. He sniffed me from head to tail and looked me in the eyes.

"Didn't end up in a bingle, didja mate? Like this ol' fella?" the dog asked, and nodded towards my father.

I had no idea what a bingle was and for some reason I couldn't quite work it out. Library? Sure. Bingle? Not a clue.

"I'm uhhh…"

The dog turned and whispered not so quietly to the rest of the pack. "Nong, this one."

"I'm sorry, what?" I asked.

"No worries mate, you'll be apples," came the response.

I wanted to say something, but I could not get even the slightest read off any of the dogs standing before me.

Rocket appeared to be trying desperately to hide a small grin. "All right, all right, that's enough," he gave in after a few more seconds.

At that, everyone began to chuckle and tails wagged.

"Don't mind Sherman here—he's never even *been* to Australia," the St. Bernard said. "My name's Duke."

"I had him for a second, though! You gotta admit the accent's getting better!" Sherman said. "Sorry about that, had to give you a little razzing, you being the son of the infamous Rocket and all that."

"Infamous, huh?" I replied.

Rocket walked over the bulldog. "And this here's Lucky."

Everyone began to snicker.

"The irony in that will be a little clearer when you hear his story," Rocket said.

Lucky grinned. "It's actually kinda funny."

"Yeah, sorry about the blocks there. Had to keep the joke running for a second," Sherman said.

"Ahh, the bingle or what have you. A car accident, right?" I replied.

Sherman nodded.

Rocket cleared his throat. "Listen fellas, now that you're here, to be honest, we could use some help."

There was a brief pause, and then all of the dogs began to chatter.

"Poor little bloke," Sherman said.

"I feel for his mother," Lucky replied.

"…out there all alone," Sherman muttered.

"So we finally get to meet Belle then?" Duke asked.

Rocket grinned. "I'm hoping she has an idea or two."

"Well, let's get a move on, then," Lucky replied.

I had to concentrate extremely hard on what had just transpired. It turns out that Rocket either told Colin's entire story to the pack, or they read him and comprehended the situation in the slightest fraction of a second. Whatever happened, they all seemed to understand and agreed to help in an instant. It was clear that they engaged in this sort of communication on a regular basis, and somehow I understood they were very accustomed to embarking on these kinds of *missions*. At least that's what they liked to call them: *missions*. I liked it.

13

Heaven Has The Best Parks

Belle was in a place everyone referred to simply as "the forest." Although I could not see anything resembling a wooded area as we walked, I had no doubt that this place was near. We passed more elaborate buildings, and just as many simple structures; not everything was designed to astound, it seemed. There were fountains here and there; man-, possibly angelic-made statues on almost every corner; and there were small push-carts with colorful tents strewn about everywhere you looked. Within these tents I saw everything from handmade clothing to toys for both humans and animals alike. There were various foods in some and artwork in others. From what I understood, if you wanted something, you simply asked for it and were on your way; all one needed was a smile and a thank you.

"Sorry about your lessons, mate," Sherman said as we walked.

"My lessons?" I asked.

"Well, yeah… You don't think you'll just know all that you suddenly do and you'll still understand it, do ya?"

"Isn't that a contradiction?"

Lucky laughed. "Life is full of contradictions, even after you die."

"What are we talking about again?" I asked.

Rocket glanced over his shoulder as we strolled past a rather large man on a red bicycle. "Usually when you come up here for the first time, you need a bit to soak it all up, you know? Get your head around things."

"I think I'll be all right."

"Of course you will. But a month or two of slow exposure for the novice is never a bad thing," Rocket replied.

"A month or two? You mean it can take that long to… to understand the things I already… understand?"

"Well, everyone's different," Rocket replied. "Just because you know how to drink water from a river, doesn't mean you truly understand the river itself."

I thought about that for a minute and then nodded.

"Get the picture?" Rocket asked.

"I think I do."

Lucky began to snicker, then Duke, followed by Sherman, and finally Rocket.

Duke shook his head, looked at me and winked. "Well, I'm glad you understood it, because no one else did."

"He's always wanted to sound prophetic, hasn't he?" Lucky asked. "Understand the river my tail!"

Rocket laughed. "I can be deep when I wanna! You shoulda heard my bit about opposable thumbs earlier!"

Duke grinned and nudged me in the shoulder. "Don't worry, new guys always get it the worst."

I nodded. "I'm beginning to see that."

"You think *we're* bad?" Sherman asked. "You should see some of the humans!"

Lucky nodded. "Yeah, they're the worst. Well, maybe not the worst, but they are pretty bad. Funny though, you gotta admit."

Duke chuckled. "I've seen fathers convince their own sons that they aren't really dead, they're just dreaming, only to break the news to 'em at a party over cake and ice cream!"

"Cake and what? Wait, I think I saw that in the grocery store."

"Ahh mate, it's the best," Sherman said. "Ben and Jerry's? Forget about it. Anyway, when they say God has a sense of humor, they weren't kidding. The practical jokes that go on around here? Insane, I tell ya."

"Seems kind of mean if you ask me. Someone telling a family member they're not really here," I said.

"Hey, sometimes the best way to deal with a traumatic experience is through a little humor, ya know?" Rocket said.

And so went the conversation as we made our way to Belle. I never asked the pack why we weren't just "wishing" our way there. At first, time seemed to be of the essence, but to everyone else it just didn't seem to matter at all. The more I thought about that, the clearer it became. When we were ready, we could go back to whatever point in time we chose. It was far more difficult for me to ignore time than it was to comprehend everything else I was experiencing. I suspect time is fickle in a way. It doesn't like to be ignored and relinquishes its grasp on a soul quite reluctantly once that soul is in no need of it.

After a while I noticed the buildings which surrounded us began to thin in number and size. It wasn't long before they shrank far into the distance. The grass road which we traveled also began to transform as we walked. The grass and flowers thinned, giving way to brightly colored gems dispersed throughout. It wasn't long before the entire path was comprised of nothing but these brilliant stones. On both sides of our new trail small, rolling hills blanketed in emerald grass stretched on for as far as I could see, but the path we traveled looked as if a rainbow had fallen to earth and now served as the most brilliantly colored road to ever grace its surface.

I found myself staring in wonder at the path as we walked. Purples, greens, reds, blues, and oranges of all shades glimmered and glistened beneath us. There were also colors that I know do not exist on earth, so it would be impossible to describe them here, but just as a small tease, know that there are sights, large and small such as this, beyond description that await you. The gems made a sort of musical sound as our paws trod over them, and the light reflecting from the path painted our coats in colorful washes of splendor. It wasn't long before I quite literally ran smack into the rear of Duke, who had stopped for one reason or another.

"I always love this spot," Duke said, ignoring my sudden impact with his backside.

I looked up from the rainbow road and saw an enormous sapphire-blue river cutting through the fields. On the far bank stood millions of impossibly large trees which stretched off to the horizon, where they met with enormous purple mountains. When I looked back down at the river, I noticed we had climbed a rather large hill which sloped all the way to its closest bank. There was no bridge anywhere that I could see, no way to cross without swimming.

"Personally, I like to fly from here," Rocket answered my question before I could ask it.

"Fly?"

Rocket winked and nodded. "Figured I'd save this lesson for this spot."

"Always one for the dramatic," Lucky said.

Rocket chuckled, and before I could say another word, a pair of enormous wings expanded behind him. My jaw plummeted, as I'm sure you can imagine. My father's wings were such a brilliant white that at first I could not look at them. As my eyes adjusted and I blinked away several tears, I began to make out their intricate outlines and what seemed to be gold and silver highlights throughout.

"This is the fun part," Rocket said through an enormous grin.

50

14

<u>Winged Flight 101</u>

Rocket walked over to where I stood mute for the second time since arriving here.

"Didn't think you'd get to Heaven and not earn your wings, did ya?" he asked.

"I didn't… I mean… I wasn't aware I was supposed to get any," I managed to stutter.

"It's easy, kid, just feel 'em. That's the best way I can describe it," Duke said.

"Yeah, it's like stretching and yawning at the same time… only you're stretching your wings, ya know?" Sherman added.

"Stretching and yawning?" Lucky asked.

"Yeah! Isn't that what it feels like to you?" Sherman replied.

Lucky thought about that for a moment. "Hmm, I guess it does. That and feelings. You know, happy thoughts."

Duke began to laugh. "Happy thoughts? Okay, Peter Pan!"

"You don't think happy thoughts when you fly?" Lucky asked.

Duke stopped mid-laugh. "I guess you're right. Touché, little buddy."

Rocket flexed his wings out over us and turned around to face the river while looking back at me over his shoulder. "Give it a shot, kiddo."

I thought about my wings, which I'd never seen or used. I thought about stretching, though I didn't know what to stretch. I thought about yawning, even though I wasn't tired. And I thought about all of the happy things I could, though I had no idea who Peter Pan was. Instantly I felt my new wings spread out behind me as if I'd had them forever and always knew how to use them. I looked over my shoulder to see that they looked very much like my father's. They shined pearly white in the sun, with hints of gold and silver mixed throughout. My father's wings, as well as mine, were so white and so bright that the multicolored brilliance of the path below our feet paled in comparison. But you can imagine the scene: a perfect cobalt blue sky above, an emerald forest below, and a sapphire river before us. I stood there with my father and new friends, completely speechless – *yet again.*

"Yep. I said the same thing when Rocket first brought me here," Sherman said, commenting on my loss for words.

Duke and Lucky nodded in agreement.

"So it's pretty simple," Rocket said. "You already know how to use your wings if you think about it. They're just a natural extension of your body, and once you start testing them out, you'll find they pretty much act on their own a lot of the time anyway."

I tried to move my wings a little, and they did as I asked.

"You sure we aren't rushing him a bit?" Duke asked.

Rocket looked at me and winked. "Oh, I think he'll surprise you."

Duke grinned and expanded his own wings. They were dark black with bright red and yellow lightning bolts extending their length. Lucky's were green and gold, while Sherman's were blue with white stars and red stripes.

"You can change their color anytime you want, mate," Sherman said, and with a loud "YAHOO!", he jogged forward and leapt off the hill, soaring high above the river below.

"See you on the other side... so to speak," Lucky said, and he, too, took to the skies.

Duke grinned, winked at me, and followed his companions into the air.

"So you ready for this? It's actually a heck of a lot of fun," Rocket said.

I nodded. I wasn't afraid by any means, but I was a little overwhelmed.

"Best thing to do is just dive right in, if you know what I mean," Rocket said, and with that, he took several quick steps and shot into the air, his wings thumping hard against the wind.

Rocket circled above while Duke, Sherman and Lucky all swooped in and around each other, calling for me to join them. I took a deep breath, ran towards the crest of the hill and jumped.... My feet left the ground, and my wings did exactly what I wished for them to, which was not let me plummet to the ground. It took no less than a fraction of a second for me to never want to walk again. The wind raced across my face and along the length of my body as if it were a long-lost friend finally greeting me after an obscenely extensive absence. The ground fell away, and the river shrank smaller and smaller with every beat of my wings. Duke rolled in the air above as if he had been born of wind and cloud, easily maneuvering into spirals and twists no bird or man-made flying machine could ever dream of duplicating. Sherman raced along behind him, trying as best he could to keep up. Lucky just circled about lazily, an enormous grin flapping away at his jowls.

"So whatcha think?" Rocket's voice asked from above and to the right of me.

Again I was at a loss for words.

"That's what I said," Rocket replied within my thoughts.

15

Heaven Needs Chefs and Bakers Too

Have you ever dreamt of flying? I've spoken with many a soul in my time, and almost all of them agree on one thing: at some point in their lives they have dreamt of such an act. The ability to soar through the heavens, touch the clouds, feel the wind on their bodies. Of course most of the birds, flying insects, and flying mammals regard the act a bit less enthusiastically, but given the choice, they too would rather have the ability than not, which makes perfect sense considering their makeup. Even when those who *can* fly, dream, they often dream of soaring through the clouds, not trotting along the earth. But if you have ever dreamt of flying, you will know what I mean when I say it is exactly the stuff from which dreams are made.

I am going to sound less heroic and far shallower than I actually am when I say this, but for quite a while that day in the sky, I forgot all about Colin and his unfortunate plight. Perhaps it was selfishness; perhaps I was just overwhelmed by all of my new surroundings and abilities; perhaps Colin gave me a brief reprieve without my knowledge. But that beautiful day in May, high above the rainbow-colored road and the forest and the river below, I truly felt as if I was in Heaven for the first time.

Our merry band of winged canines swooped and soared through the sky, hooting and howling the entire time. Rocket engaged in aerial acrobatics that rivaled Duke's, while Sherman continued to do his best to keep up. I myself even managed a few tricks and grew quite comfortable following my father and Duke in whatever maneuver they attempted. Lucky, however, was content to close his eyes and circle lazily below us, the smile spread across his face never once faltering.

After a time—I honestly cannot recall how long it was—we struck out across the forest. I was amazed to see how many people and animals dotted the woodland floor when it came into view. Occasionally I spied a small house or dwelling of sorts. There were tiny streams which connected both large and small lakes throughout. High above the trees, several humans soared on wings of their own. When they spotted us, they would smile and wave. I could hear voices wishing us luck on our journey and hoping the best for Colin. I was still getting used to everyone knowing what I was thinking when Rocket began circling above a small valley.

"Belle's here," he said I as glided next to him.

I couldn't see beneath the canopy of leaves. "Is James with her?"

"Yes, and so is your grandmother,"

Above us, Duke, Lucky and Sherman circled, awaiting a signal from Rocket.

"What's the fella say? Looks like Belle's down there," Sherman asked in my mind's ear.

"Sherman's asking what's next," I said.

"Yeah, I heard him too," Rocket replied. "Let's go down, then."

With that, we dove towards the ground and glided beneath the emerald canopy. The forest floor sloped down towards a powerful river, which bent and wove its way into a small, mist-shrouded valley. Rocket led the way, gliding over several waterfalls and deep, cobalt pools. The forest smelled of earth, timber, and damp leaves. Where the sun was able to penetrate the natural umbrella, yellow rays of light glittered to the ground like columns of warm gold. No dream could ever aspire to be as beautiful.

Rocket landed in a small clearing of bizarre fruit trees the likes of which I'd never seen. Of course at the time, I think I'd only ever seen an apple tree and a peach tree, maybe a picture of a coconut tree, but these were different; these trees bore a multitude of different fruits *each*.

"I don't think I've been to this part of the forest," Lucky said when he landed.

I looked over at the bulldog and watched as his wings simply faded from sight. I was surprised to glance over my own shoulder and notice mine dissolving as well. Duke and Sherman landed near us and began sniffing about. They too were here for the first time and seemed pleased to be exploring a new area.

"I've heard of this place," Duke said as he glanced up at the unusual fruit trees.

"Looks like Belle's further down in the valley," Rocket said.

Sherman began wagging his tail. "I smell food."

Indeed, the smell of food began wafting up from the valley not far below. The scent was of obvious human design and with that, let me take this opportunity to comment on human food and what humans think we canines enjoy. First, allow me to say this. *Dog food is bland.* It's not exciting. It's not even entertaining. We eat it, and we appear to enjoy it because for most of us that's all we generally receive. It is what it is. If you think it's what we truly enjoy, what we prefer, and what we

55

absolutely adore, I suggest this. The next time you have a juicy pear, or a perfectly baked loaf of bread, even a plate of pasta covered in tangy tomato sauce (I won't even mention the prospect of cheese), place said meal next to your pet's bowl of usual, predictable cuisine. You'll have your answer within a fraction of a frantic, lip-smacking second.

Now I don't add this to berate dog food designers or the multitudes of owners who hand out said provisions to their beloved canine, but to give a brief insight to a pet's affection for variety. So now you might be a little more understanding when we appear to beg for whatever delicacy adorns your plate or table from time to time.

"Why is it humans always make the best food?" Sherman asked.

"Depends on the human, I guess," Duke replied. "I had my share of slop in my time."

Sherman nodded. "It's no wonder humans have such a fascination with it. If I had grown up cooking like that, I'd be obsessed by it too. It's too bad they can't enjoy it like we can, what with our superior senses and all."

Rocket turned to Sherman. "You don't cook? I thought you did?"

Sherman looked embarrassed. "I dabble."

"You gotta try baking sometime," Lucky said, and licked his lips. "Nothing smells better than baked bread in the mornings."

Duke nodded. "He's right. I've been over to his place when he's baking, and it's incredible."

I was puzzled. "You...you're telling me that you all cook?"

"Sure, why not?" Rocket replied. "Beats just wishing for something; more fun, too."

"I haven't tried yet, but I'm going to set up a nice kitchen soon," Duke replied.

I laughed. "You must be joking. You're kidding me again, right?"

"Why do you keep thinking so many things are impossible? Haven't you seen or done enough to understand nothing is beyond your reach anymore?" Duke asked.

"Lessons, mate..." Sherman whispered.

"It's just...I never thought I'd...well, I never thought I'd have a conversation about cooking with another animal. I never thought I'd have a conversation about cooking at all!"

"You keep saying animals and humans, humans and animals. We need to break you of that habit," Lucky replied. "Anyway, you show me a dog, and I'll show you an aspiring chef."

"Well, maybe not all of 'em," Duke added.

Lucky chuckled. "Well, yeah, not all of 'em."

"Okay, enough culinary conversations," Rocket said. "Let's get a move on."

16
A Reason To Celebrate

We made our way into the valley by following the river and a small path that had been laid there. As we descended, the air grew cooler and thicker with smells. Not only was the scent of the very forest stronger here, but we were obviously approaching many humans and animals alike. It wasn't long before the sounds of music and quite a lot of laughter echoed up the hill towards us.

For those of you reading this tale who might not be as familiar with canines as you'd like, know this. It may sound strange, but we *do* laugh. We might not understand or comprehend all things human before we find ourselves in the hereafter, but we do possess a sense of humor that rivals most every other animal I have ever met, including humans. Now apes? That lot has a sense of humor only rivaled by James, if you catch my meaning. They can find humor in almost every situation without fail. It's an endearing quality we should all aspire to possess.

Rocket stopped us on an outcrop of purplish stone which overlooked the valley floor. The river cascaded over several small artificial walls and came to a slow, peaceful crawl through the center of the dale. Quaint houses and various buildings dotted the clearing. On both sides of the river, a festive celebration of sorts was in full swing, or would be soon by the looks of it.

"Elves!" Lucky said, and began wagging his tail.

"Thought it smelled like their cooking," Duke replied.

"What are elves? I mean…Who are the elves?" I asked.

"They're faeries… of sorts anyway," Rocket replied.

"I used to see 'em in the summer where I lived. Only at night, though," Sherman said.

"A few of 'em used to live by the lake on my old property," Duke said. "Nice enough people. Always willing to share whatever they had when I'd venture down to see 'em. Best cooks I ever met."

I looked closer at the group of humans dotting the landscape. Most of them did appear different than what I'd seen before; I took these for the elves. They were taller and more slender on average, and the majority of them wore long white hair, which actually appeared silver in the golden sunlight.

"Did you ever see them? Before, I mean?" Rocket asked of me.

"I'm not sure. They *do* look familiar, though," I replied.

"Yeah, I wasn't sure," Rocket said. "I never knew any to live near you. But ya never know. They travel all the time. Never in any one place for very long. At least not down there. Up here they're far more comfortable... as they should be."

"Let's get on then, mates," Sherman said. "I'm starved."

We made our way down the remaining path and were greeted by several children playing near the water's edge. We all received pats on the head and scratches behind the ears. Lucky was even rolled over and scratched on the belly for a minute or two.

"The kids always like the smaller dogs," Duke said, and snickered. Lucky seemed indifferent to the jibe.

"You guys go on and grab something to eat; Tucker and I are going to go find Belle first," Rocket said.

From somewhere in the crowd, another dog as well as several adult humans pointed towards us and passed the word that we were finally here, as if we had been expected for some time.

I trotted up beside Rocket. "Did you hear that? Someone said we're *finally* here..."

"Yep."

"I didn't know we were expected."

Rocket chuckled a little. "You'll get the hang of all this soon enough."

As we made our way into the center of the festivities, I noticed the river was being filled with tiny floating orange candles. They smelled of vanilla and cinnamon as they burned.

"I wonder what the celebration is about," I asked.

"Well, read one of them. See what you think."

"So you already know, then?" I asked.

"Yep," Rocket said.

I closed my eyes for a moment as we walked and concentrated on the many minds surrounding us. The humans, elves, and animals alike all seemed focused on one thing. *My mother.*

"It's a party for Belle?" I asked.

"Keep looking," Rocket said.

I closed my eyes again, careful not to bump into anyone as I walked. It wasn't really that hard, I just knew where to go without having to see. The thoughts I received were all focused on Belle, but behind that, there was more. Belle was the last daughter in a long line of children going back well over a hundred years. My grandmother was here, her mother, and so on and so on for generation after generation. Evidently, a line of mothers as long as Belle's was something to celebrate, which explained the multitude of decorations and festive revelers.

Many of my brothers, cousins, and so forth were also spread about the valley. It turned out that all but just a few of my entire lineage was present. It was an enormous number, and the magnitude of this was not lost on me. I was anxious to meet each one of them—as soon as Colin was able to do the same, of course. Again I felt a deep sadness for the boy but tried to concentrate on the immediate situation.

"Does this happen a lot?" I asked.

"All the time," Rocket replied. "It is a good excuse for a party, yeah? I mean your mother and her mother and so on and so on have been around for a long time, ya know."

"Wow. So this is like a big *thank you*?"

"Yep. James should be here somewhere. He never misses one of these."

I looked around but did not see Him.

"We lucked out on the timing," Rocket said. "I wish Colin could be here for this though. He'd like it, I'm sure."

"I was just thinking the same thing."

"I know."

"Can't we just, I dunno, bring him back to this point later?" I asked.

"Well… not really, no. Time travel and all that fun stuff only works when you're talking about the living. I always hate that term. *The living*. Sounds so… I dunno, like we're not really here, doesn't it?"

I nodded.

"I mean, this is living too, isn't it? Anyway, don't get me started; I could spend hours on that."

"Are you two ready?" a voice asked from just ahead.

I looked up and spotted Belle. Beside her stood another female dog that I did not recognize, but I instantly understood she was my grandmother. James now stood beside them. He held a drink of sorts in one hand and wore a funny-looking hat which I had noticed several of the children wearing earlier.

"Hello, Belle. Hello, Rose," Rocket said as we walked over. "James, you don't mind if we borrow the guests of honor for a while, do you?"

James laughed and shook his head. "Rocket, does it look like we're going anywhere? We haven't even started the games yet, much less broken into the elven wine!"

"Ahh, they brought their wine, did they?" Rocket replied.

James nodded. "When don't they? It's supposed to be a new blend from what I understand. I'm excited to sample it."

"So this is Pickle, then, is it?" Rose asked, and smiled. She was a large dog, part Husky and part Doberman from what I could tell.

"He goes by Tucker now," Belle whispered, trying to suppress a small grin.

"Pickle is fine, ma'am," I replied. "It's very nice to meet you."

Rose circled me and wagged her tail. "I've looked in on you since you were a puppy, Tucker, and I have to say, you turned out just fine."

"Thank you."

"So are you two ready?" Belle asked.

I almost asked how Belle knew what we were here to ask of her, but it made sense before I could form the words.

Rocket and I nodded.

"I filled them in a little," James said. "I do appreciate your help in this matter."

My grandmother looked over our shoulders. "I see you brought Duke, Sherman, and Lucky again," she said. "They seem to be pretty good in a pinch. I hope they learned their lesson from last time, though."

"Lesson?" I asked. "Last time?"

"Long story," Rose answered. "Let's just say these things can go, well, they can go bad. Not that I'm blaming those boys, but…. Well, I'll save that story for another time. No need to frighten you your first time out!"

Bad. My grandmother's use of the word alarmed me. Even James seemed affected by the word, and a sad, almost desperate look fell over him for a moment.

I tried to break the awkward heaviness in the air. "So you've, you've been on this sort of…."

"…mission?" Rose asked. "Is that what they are still calling them?"

"Yes, ma'am."

Rose laughed. "Oh, I've been doing this sort of thing for a looong time. Who do you think taught Rocket all of his moves?"

"Okay, okay…" Rocket interrupted. "Let's get down there and bring this boy home! I can't enjoy this party until we do."

"Looks like the fellas are ready," Belle said, and motioned.

Behind us, flanked by half a dozen small children, Duke, Sherman, and Lucky trotted down the path. They now had flowers and colorful leaves braided into their coats courtesy of the throng of children we had passed.

"We ready to fly?" Sherman asked as they approached.

We all nodded, and James' smile returned. Colin's assortment of four-footed guardian angels was on the way.

17
<u>Hearts Big And Small</u>

Everyone arrived simultaneously at the shelter which housed Ginger and her new litter. Rocket decided that we should fly versus just wishing our way there, which was nice, not to mention a bit more exciting. It also gave us ample time to go over his ideas with the pack, as well as consider options and opinions from everyone. By the time we landed, we had a pretty good idea of what to do. We weren't one hundred percent positive of our plans, but in theory it all sounded good.

" okay, ladies. Are you ready for your bit?" Rocket asked.

Belle and Rose nodded and walked through one of the kennel's closest walls. I heard Rose whisper to my mother that she always hated seeing what they were about to, but that it was nice knowing they could help.

Rocket watched them go and turned to face the rest of us. "Okay, fellas, this is where we part. Duke, Sherman, Lucky, you all know what to do. Tucker and I will head off in search of Colin. Let me know if you have any issues, or if something doesn't go to plan."

"Right mate, we're on it," Sherman said. "Just like old times!"

"You just be careful," Duke added and when he did, a serious, and somewhat disconcerting look fell over his face. "I mean it. Something tells me you need to watch your back. So do what I said and *be careful.*"

"Come on, ya dilly-dallyers!" Sherman said and leapt into the air, darting towards the clouds above.

"I guess we're flying then," Duke said as he watched Sherman speed away.

"Good day for it at least," Lucky replied. "See you soon."

Duke and Lucky took to the air and vanished over the tree line.

"Fly or pop?" Rocket asked when we were alone.

"Pop? Oh you mean wish our way there?" I asked.

"Yep. Can't remember how or why we started calling it that," Rocket replied.

"Let's fly," I said.

"That's my boy."

The thing about winged flight in the hereafter is this. Just like wishing your way to a specific location or time, you can do the same thing in flight. You travel as *fast* as you'd like and arrive *when* you'd like as well. Everyone had agreed on our timing, as it was directly related to Ginger's litter. Two of her small pups would not live through the night, and it was crucial that Belle and Rose were there for them.

"It does seem like the longest day you've ever had, doesn't it?" I heard Rocket ask.

"Yes, it does. Still takes a little getting used to."

"It will get easier. You're doing fine, by the way."

"Thank you," I replied. *"So how many of these... missions have you been on?"*

"This makes two thousand and seventy seven," Rocket answered.

I was flabbergasted. *"Two thousand? How in the world have you had the time to...?"* I stopped myself.

I heard Rocket begin to laugh aloud over the wind racing between us. *"See? You're starting to understand things!"*

"Does everyone do these sorts of things? You know, this sort of mission or what have you?"

"Not everyone, no, but many do; all the time. They're always different, ya know. Sometimes it's as simple as delivering a message. Sometimes these outings require an entire brigade of angels and months, sometimes years of effort."

"So is that what we are? Angels?"

"Of sorts, sure."

"Are there, you know... bad ones? Bad angels, I mean?"

"What does your heart tell you?"

"I   feel   like   there   are."

"Then there you go."

"Will we see any?"

"Today? I'm not sure. Tomorrow? Who knows. Eventually? Yep."

This concerned me more than anything I had learned thus far. *"What do we do if we see one, or some of them?"*

"We'll deal with that when and if the time comes. For now, don't think about it. Focus on Colin," Rocket replied. *"Seems Duke and the boys have found his parents' house,"* he added a second later.

"What about Belle and Rose? How are they doing?" I asked.

My grandmother's voice whispered in my mind before Rocket could reply. *"Ginger is doing well, but it won't be long for the two smallest."*

I knew that two of the puppies were not long of this earth, but I was still saddened by it. It seemed such a waste for a newborn to die. I did not understand then that sometimes souls aren't always meant to stay in one place for very long.

"We're here. Looks like Dave and Rebecca have headed back home," Rocket said.

I looked down and saw Pleasant Grove far below. Beneath the canopy of trees, the river glistened in the afternoon light like a gold and orange road spun from glass. Rocket and I descended to the beach where my family had spent the day.

"He's getting tired, which is a good thing," Rocket said, and turned his gaze down the shore.

"Tired? What do you mean?"

"I mean he's been here a very long time. And no matter how much a soul refuses its fate, eventually it grows weary of being alone. Tired, if you will. Our little visit to him earlier got him thinking."

It made sense to me, but I guessed I only understood some of what my father was saying. Of course, I understand more now than I did then, *far* more to be frank. Colin was not a bad soul. He had no ill-will towards others and not a hint of malice tainted his heart. He was a good soul and kind. In life he was a loving and caring child. It made sense that after a time he would long to love and be loved again.

"Is he here? I can't really sense him," I asked.

Rocket nodded. "Oh, he's here, all right. He's watching us."

With that, I scanned the tree line and river bank. I did not spot the boy.

Rocket took a few steps down the beach, his eyes stopping on an enormous raspberry bush. "Hello, Colin," he said. "I have some news that you might like. We found Ginger today! *And* she's had puppies!"

There was no answer.

"But I suspect you knew that already…." Rocket added.

For several minutes I saw nothing but the raspberry bush, and the shadows beyond. I heard nothing but the sounds of the river gurgling and the birds singing in the distance. Then, here and there I began to notice small glimmers of light. After a moment Colin appeared. And he was not alone.

18

Not All Dogs Go to Heaven

Standing beside Colin was the largest canine I had ever seen. His head towered over the small boy's, dwarfing both Rocket and I. His coat was a pure black shadow. His eyes were an icy blue. Perched high on his back, a pair of sleek black wings seemed to defy the sunlight as if they had no need of it now, nor ever.

"I said they would return. Did I not?" the strange dog said, and looked down to Colin.

Rocket smiled, which was something I hardly expected. This was the first time in this new life that I had even considered being afraid for myself. And I could tell Rocket's smile was only skin deep; he was terrified.

"Hello, Drake," Rocket said, and stepped towards the two.

"Rocket," the beast of a dog replied, and bowed his head slightly. As he did, he grinned, but it was not a welcoming smile in the least.

I could read nothing from the strange creature. No thoughts, no emotions, not a thing. But somewhere in my mind I knew to be frightened, not only for myself but for Colin. I understood that there was a *very* real danger present.

"Have you been bothering our friend here?" Rocket asked.

"*Your* friend? Surely you jest?" Drake replied. His voice was deep, almost cavernous; you could feel it deep in your chest and stomach. "Colin and I have known each other for quite some time now. Isn't that so, lad?"

Colin turned, looked up at Drake and then back to Rocket. He nodded but remained quiet.

"And I guess you've been filling his head with all that 'You didn't have to die and nobody wants you anymore and death is a punishment' dribble-drabble the entire time?" Rocket asked.

Drake's false grin vanished in an instant. He stared at Rocket and I for a moment and then slowly, his smiled reappeared, this time even brighter and with far more teeth.

"Dribble-drabble, you say?" Drake asked. "If I'm so full of this, what did you call it, dribble and drabble, then would you mind explaining to my small friend here why his life was stolen from him at such a young and promising age?"

Rocket sighed but continued to smile as he looked at the tiny boy. "Colin, do you feel like your life was taken away? I mean really *taken* away? I don't know about you, but I feel more alive now than I ever have."

Colin turned his gaze to the river but remained silent. His hand fluttered near his temple again and Rocket winced just slightly; it was a small reaction, but I noticed it.

Drake raised one enormous paw and placed it on Colin's left shoulder. "Come then, lad. We both know what we need to know about your past, what happened here, and all about your parents and their negligence. Let's leave these two to spread their deception elsewhere."

Rocket laughed. "Deception? Colin, do you think I'm lying to you? What does your heart say?"

Colin looked back to my father, then to me and then to Drake. "I don't think you're lying."

Rocked winked. "That's because I'm not."

Drake looked down to Colin and growled. "You were killed at the place you loved more than any other, Colin! MURDERED right there in that river you so cherished! Who would do such a thing to a child so young?" he asked. The dog's voice echoed through the forest and out over the water. "Who would destroy such a beautiful life? Who wouldn't protect it in the first place? I will tell you who wouldn't do those things. *Me*! And I am telling you now, these two misguided fools are *not* your friends."

Colin seemed to shrink beneath the weight of Drake's anger. His hands began to shake, and his lower lip trembled. Rocket appeared visibly shaken now and somehow, for some reason I could not ascertain, he appeared to be in considerable pain.

"We could lose him," Rocket's voice whispered in my mind. It seemed labored, as if he were struggling to keep his thoughts between the two of us. A sense of agony echoed behind his words.

Drakes grin widened. "Think on it, Colin. The adventures you *could* have had. The times you *could* have spent with your mother, your father, your new baby brother which they have conceived to replace you! Ask yourself… why would someone rob you of such things? Why would they want to hurt you so? How could your parents replace you so easily? You've never been unkind to a single soul your life!" Drake paused and then added, "As short as it was."

I whispered to Rocket with my mind. *"What do we do?"*

"What do you do?" Drake replied allowed. He'd somehow managed to hear me. "What do YOU do?" The dog repeated and looked directly into my eyes. "You? You stop lying to yourself! You stop lying to poor Colin here! You tell him the truth of it! You tell him that he died on a slippery rock back there because no one cared! NO ONE! Not YOU," Drake looked to the sky "...not Him, not even Colin's mother and father who sat idly by!"

"ENOUGH!" Rocket shouted and lunged across the beach, teeth exposed, eyes afire.

Drake didn't so much as flinch. He simply laughed as my father was suddenly thrown backwards just as he reached the giant dog, as if he'd collided with an invisible wall. There was a loud snap, and Rocket's head tilted skywards in a howl of utter and complete anguish. I saw fear flash within my father's eyes then, total and terrible fear.

The two had barely come close to physical contact, yet my father had reacted to something tangible, something solid. Though I could not see what, I felt it. Drake's will, his utter complete conviction, had risen up and met Rocket as if it were alive.

"I don't want to be here anymore!" Colin said; tears now streamed down his cheeks.

I watched as Drake stepped over my father's writhing body and stole a sidelong glance in my direction. He grinned at me. It was then, for a fraction of a second, that I caught a glimpse of Drake's past and saw a lifetime of horrific battles. Wars he'd been forced into year after terrifying year. I was immediately thankful Rocket had not engaged in such a fight. Drake would have beaten him easily in a physical confrontation.

The huge black dog circled Colin, who now stood shaking and wringing his hands. "No, of course you don't want to be here anymore, lad. And I for one don't blame you," he said. "Come with me and I promise you, unlike these two fools, I will NEVER lie to you."

I didn't know what to do. Fear the likes of which I had never experienced and never even imagined possible gripped my entire being. Harsh and terrible images raced into my mind, forcing me to understand things I not only reviled, but wished I had never known. Impressions of lost, wondering souls walking the earth and far beyond, slashed into my thoughts as if made of the sharpest glass. A tangible web of despair connected these souls, and worse, hatred mixed with regret mixed with remorse so vivid, so passionately alive that it seemed no amount of effort could ever cleanse those it bound together. And now, that terrible web was reaching out to touch me. I was horrified.

"We could lose him, Tucker. We could lose him forever!" Rocket's voice echoed into my thoughts. *"It can happen. It has happened. Lost souls, doomed souls. I've seen it. I've lost them! If they chose to go, to be no more, there's nothing anyone, not you, not I, not even James can do about it! We can't let this happen! We...."*

I looked to my father who now lay crumpled on the beach, his breathing labored, his face twisted in misery. He seemed old then, fragile—desperate. The light once dancing in his eyes was now clouded.

"What do I do?" I asked.

Rocket's voice came into my thoughts, but I could not make out the words. All I heard were desperate cries of pain. I tried to reach out to Belle and the others, to anyone, but was greeted by terrible, total silence, as if the world outside had vanished into nothingness.

The terror which gripped me had talons now and they plunged into me. It was so real, so painful and so true that to this day I shudder to think on that fear. I knew there was a horrifying, powerful soul before me and that not only was I in danger, very real, very genuine danger, but so was poor Colin. I was more frightened for the boy than myself. Part of me wanted to run, to hide, and to whisk away from this new nightmare, but I was frozen. I screamed in my mind until I could take it no longer.

I don't know how, but I stepped in front of Rocket. My limbs shook, and I did everything I could to hide it. "Colin," I started, my voice quivering, "I don't know this, this Drake character. And I don't know why he claims to be your friend, as I'm almost certain he is not." I swallowed hard and cleared my throat. "I'm rather new here myself, to be honest." My words came in stuttering jolts. I was nervous and terrified to do any more harm to the boy. But I was determined, afraid yes, but determined. "I know we've only just met, but I'd like to be your friend, and I'd like to help you, especially with this Drake fellow and others of his kind."

"My kind?" the enormous dog asked. He then let out a very long, very sinister laugh. "What makes you think that we are any different, young pup? Hmmm? My kind? You ARE my kind! And my kind have been here since before you were born, before your father's father was born and before his! We have always been, and we shall forever be! We are timeless, and we are far more powerful than you can dream."

"And modest, too," I replied, ignoring the dog's obvious fury and frightening insinuations. I then turned my eyes back to the small boy, ignoring Drake as best I could. "I guess what I'm trying to say, Colin, is this. I'm very new here myself. You have been here far longer than me, but if I've understood anything today, it's that this Drake gent means you no good, and I can't bear to allow him near you any longer."

"ALLOW ME?" Drake roared. His voice shook the earth beneath my feet and the air around me. "ALLOW ME? Who do you think you are? YOU? You are going to ALLOW me?"

I stared at the giant and for the first time, I felt no fear whatsoever. "No," I responded. "I will not allow it, Drake."

The dog lunged over Colin and raced across the beach towards Rocket and I. He came to within a mere inch of me before stopping.

"Careful there, Drake, he's a wild one," Rocket said, as he stumbled to his feet. "I'd watch it if I were you."

Drake's anger radiated from him, especially his eyes. His breath was rancid and searing hot, but he did not frighten me any longer. Broken and terribly fragmented images of the dog had raced into my mind, but were torn away almost as quickly by a force I could not understand. But they had been enough that I began to feel sorry for him.

"You would be wise to warn your son of me," Drake said without ever taking his eyes from mine.

"You know what, Drake? This is getting boring," Rocket replied. "It's always the same with you. Rage this, anger that, lackluster unoriginal threats, blah blah blah. Leave this poor boy alone and go find some meaning in your life. I dunno; chase your tail, howl at the moon, something—ANYTHING! Whatever it is you do when you're not busy being miserable."

Drake glared at my father and then glanced back to Colin. He stood there for a moment just staring at the boy. "You can't save all of them, these lost ones," he said without turning back to us.

Colin's expression had changed. The fear was gone, even the sadness was gone. There in place of both seemed to now exist a small glimmer of hope. My heart swelled with it.

"Some will never wish to be found," Drake said and just like that, he faded from sight.

Rocket sighed and walked towards Colin. He shook once or twice as if shedding the last vestiges of considerable pain he'd appeared to have endured. "Well, that was fun!"

70

Colin smiled for what could have been the first time in many, many years.

19

<u>Victory Is Never Guaranteed</u>

When I asked Rocket earlier if there were others like us, only opposite, I had no idea we were flying straight towards one of the worst my father had ever met. Drake was and still is a fine example of how horrific and how damaged a soul can become. He is not the worst I have encountered, but he was the first, and the meeting continues to haunt me to this day.

I've spoken many times to James and others regarding the likes of Drake and their effects on souls like Colin. There have been wars fought between both sides since the beginning of time. I'd like to say we always win, but that would not be true. Sometimes a soul may chose to remain lost forever, sometimes not. But in the end we will always be there to try and help, regardless of the dangers we face or the outcome. We will always try. Colin was my first victory in that ongoing battle, and I am proud to have written of it now.

Since that day on the riverbank, I have encountered Drake and his ilk numerous times. They have eluded me on occasion, but I and others like me have managed to curb their effects whenever we learn of them. We've even managed to help a few. After all, that is why we are here; well, that and chocolate.

When I first encountered Drake and learned of others like him, I wanted nothing to do with them. If I *never* saw him in particular again, it would have been far too soon. But now, he is at the top of my list, my "mission impossible," if you will. After all, everyone needs saving at one point in their lives—or afterlives. And regardless of how Drake feels about the matter, I will never give up on him. Somewhere deep in the place where his heart used to be, I believe Drake knows this, and longs for a hero, though he would never admit it—not yet anyway, and especially not to me.

Rocket and I managed to draw Colin out of his seclusion over the next several hours. We watched as the sun retreated over the horizon and a brilliantly illuminated moon took its place. Colin's mood seemed to brighten with every passing moment, and he was excited to learn that Ginger had been found and was safe.

Duke, Sherman, and Lucky were successful in their mission as well. When they appeared on the beach where Colin, Rocket and I sat, they were full of good news.

"We finally found it!" Sherman said as they landed.

"I'm pretty sure we woke the entire neighborhood trying to get that collar out of the desk, but we managed it," Duke said.

Lucky landed a few seconds later with said item held tight in his jaws.

Rocket smiled and wagged his tail. "Good work, fellas! Colin, these are the boys. Boys, this is Colin."

Colin grinned. "You were at my parent's house?" he asked the trio of dogs.

Lucky nodded and walked over to where the boy stood. He placed the collar on the ground at his feet and beamed. "We had to get *this* for you."

Colin picked up the collar and studied it. "Ginger," he said after a moment. "I picked this one out. I liked the red and blue in it."

"We know. And the best part is, you asked your parents to put their e-mail address on it in case you ever moved," Lucky replied.

"How did you know that?" Colin asked.

"I'll tell you what, Colin," Rocket interrupted. "There's a lot you need to learn, but first things first! Ginger needs your help, and that collar is how we're going to get it for her."

"It is?" Colin asked.

"Yep! But first how would you like to ride on ol' Duke here?"

Colin grinned and turned to the giant St. Bernard. "I, ummm…." he began.

Duke laughed and walked over to where the boy stood. "It's like riding a bike! Only with lots of fur."

Colin laughed. "I can ride on top of you to see Ginger?"

"Sure can, cowboy!" Duke replied. "Climb on up, and watch the upholstery."

20

<u>Lost And Found</u>

When Duke leapt into the air, Colin cheered and laughed with utter delight. I am certain I have never heard more magnificent sounds over Pleasant Grove since. If I ever choose to take up painting, I will attempt to recreate the sight of Colin riding atop Duke, his giant black wings glowing under the silver moon. I hope I do it justice.

When we landed at the shelter, Colin was all smiles. Belle and Rose were waiting on us with two bundles of excited energy. Ginger's two pups were like nothing I had ever seen. They were not the tiny balls of pink helplessness I had imagined, but larger and livelier packages of joy. They both shined in the night as if their fur was made of pure moonlight. Colin was ecstatic with their arrival and agonized with the two of them as to what their names should be. Eventually they decided on Tiki and Kaleb; fine names for excellent pups.

My mother and grandmother told Colin that they would take the new puppies and wait for him until he was done here. Colin was sad to see them leave but promised to be quick, which the pups were excited to hear.

"It was nice meeting you, Colin," Belle said.

"Yes, it was. You seem like a very nice young man," Rose added.

"Thank you," Colin replied. "And thank you for watching Tiki and Kaleb."

"You are very welcome, Colin," the two answered.

We watched as Belle, Rose and the puppies faded into the shadows.

"So would you like to see Ginger first?" Rocket asked.

"Yes, please," Colin answered. He gripped Ginger's collar tight.

"We'll wait out here, mate," Sherman said.

Colin turned to face me. "Can you come?" he asked. His smile had gone, and he looked nervous.

"Of course," I replied.

We made our way through the closest wall and found ourselves amidst rows and rows of sleeping animals. Tall metal cages ran the length of the building and within each, two, sometimes three dogs slept. The room was shrouded in darkness with only small amounts of moonlight to guide us along. A bright red exit sign near the rear of the building helped a little.

"Can they see us?" Collin whispered.

"No. Not unless you want them to," I replied.

Colin nodded. "Okay."

We found Ginger in one of the last cages near the exit. She had the entire cage to herself, as her new pups had just arrived. I was happy to see that Tiki's and Kaleb's poor little bodies had been removed. It would have been an unnecessary sight for the boy.

"Hi, girl," Colin whispered, and stepped through the metal cage.

Rocket and I waited outside and sat in silence. Colin crouched down beside his old friend and rested a hand on her shoulders as she slept. He rubbed her back and neck and kissed the top of her head for quite some time.

"I'm going to get you home, girl," he said after a while. "You and your new puppies. And don't worry about Kaleb and Tiki. I'll take good care of them, you'll see."

If I told you I refrained from shedding a tear, I'd be lying. I knew everything was going to turn out fine, but the sight of little Colin finding his beloved Ginger after so long was just too much for dry eyes to bear.

When Colin was ready, he placed Ginger's collar around her neck, never waking her in the process. In the morning someone would make the discovery and no doubt marvel over how it could have been missed. Colin's parents would be notified, and Ginger would find her way home at long last.

"Would you like to see your parents now?" I asked as Colin left the cage.

"Yes, please," he said, and wiped away several tears of his own.

21

Healing

Duke seemed happy to have Colin on his back again and was more than willing to help the boy shed some of the sorrow he'd brought back from within the pound. Rocket and I both watched as Duke swirled round and about, performing wide swooping maneuvers, much to Colin's delight. The sight also helped Rocket and I dry our eyes as well as lighten our hearts. By the time we reached Colin's parents' home, the boy was laughing hysterically. Duke is an angel, of that there is no doubt.

When we arrived, I asked Colin if he would like someone to accompany him inside. He thanked me but declined, and I was glad for it. Not that I wouldn't have gone with him, or that any one of us would have been reluctant to support him, but because it reassured me that for the first time in quite a while, the young boy was healing. We waited for a short time, content to enjoy the night air and stars above. When Colin returned, he was smiling.

"I told them I'd be back to check on them every single day," he said.

"As you should, mate! You've got a little brother coming soon, too!" Sherman replied.

Colin's eyes sparkled. "I know!"

"So are you ready for some cake and ice cream?" Lucky asked.

Rocket laughed. "You and your cake and ice cream."

"They have ice cream?" Colin asked.

"Every flavor you can possibly imagine," Lucky replied.

So with the promise of sweets and more, we were off yet again.

22
<u>The Beginning</u>

I have spent a great deal of time with Colin and the others since this story took place. We have traveled the world together, embarked on numerous adventures and rescued souls in need, countless times. I have seen things I never dreamt possible and done things I never imagined I could. But alas, those are adventures for another time, and I will have them put to paper very soon. I can't inundate Dave with too many ideas, you know! Besides, he has a few stories of his own to pen without needing me to put thoughts into his head. I do pride myself in knowing he considers this tale an entirely original piece from his own imagination. It makes him feel good, and that's what I'm here for, though I must confess, he did lend a hand more so than he realizes.

Since that day in May I have never regretted a single moment, nor taken for granted a single event, no matter how trivial I might have considered it when I was alive. I hope my story helps you do the same.

I did return to Pleasant Grove after my mother's festival. I went alone and I lay back down beside Rebecca, my head in her lap. I traveled back to the same point in time when James had come to introduce himself and was happy to watch Dave attempt to coax Chanook back into the water again. I comforted my family, guarded their hearts, and smiled at the day. It could not have been a more perfect one.

~The End~

This Dog's Afterlife
Continues!

The following is a special **"sneak peek"** into the world of
This Dog's Afterlife
Book 2.

Enjoy!

Not All Angels Wear Halos

This Dog's Afterlife

Book 2

By
David S. Shockley II

Copyright© David S. Shockley II

For the dogs owned by animals
and the people who try and save them.

A Tale of Two Lives

"It is a far, far better thing that I do, than I have ever done; it is a far, far better rest that I go to than I have ever known." Have you ever thought back to a moment in time and wished you had said or done a particular thing? I wish I had known Dickens' work during my first short life. I would have almost certainly used that wonderful line as I lay dying. Instead, I think I muttered something far less profound, far less prophetic and far less eloquent. I believe it sounded something like, "Mmmpfh."

My name is Drake. I have endured more pain, more suffering, and more terror than you shall ever know. I have also reveled in inflicting said hardships tenfold on those whom I deem worthy. There are some that disagree with my methods. There are some who abhor them. And there are some who are terrified by them. I am quite good at what I do. I daresay I am the one of the best!

When I was born, my mother was taken from me within weeks. I never knew my father. I was packaged up like a present of sorts and carted off to my new home. I use the word *home* loosely, as I have never been able to associate any description of where I lived then with any definition of home in the least. But for the sake of storytelling, I shall use the word.

My owner was a creature of loathing. But allow me to take a moment to communicate my disgust on the term: *owner*. I have never felt that I was owned or that I was but a piece of property. However, as this human, for lack of a better word, came no closer to being what I define as family than say a flame thrower is to a kitten, I shall call him owner. His name, however, was Pathetic. In all truthfulness it was Daryl, but as I feel creatures as dimwitted as he should not possess proper names, I am fond of referring to him as Pathetic. But for you, dear reader, and again for the sake of storytelling, Pathetic shall be henceforth denoted as Daryl.

Daryl was a quite enormous, laughable man. He was fond of his own voice and used it far more than any creature who heard it wished for him to do so. I have seen millions of humans to date, and I dare say that Daryl was by far the most hideous. If I were to give him any credit at all, it would be this. He was comfortable enough with his own repulsiveness to inflict it upon others quite often. Daryl was rarely alone and displayed his horrid form to many a soul by traveling, in the open, unmasked, very, very often. There should be a law.

I was twelve weeks old when this human bought me. I refuse to say adopted as that expresses a desire to protect and nourish. Daryl *bought* me with no such intentions. He took me to his pitiful excuse for a home, placed me in a rusting steel cage only slightly larger than myself and proceeded to force two more unfortunate souls inside the prison with me. They too were pups, only of different breeds. We were never given names, only numbers.

I spent the next four weeks within that miniature Hell. I never once stepped outside of it. Seven and Eight (the two other pups confined with me) endured the same discomfort. As a result, we fought each other often, which of course Daryl had planned. We slept when we could under the hot August sun and clashed at night when the weather was cool enough to allow us a release of frustration. We were fed at the same time out of the same dish, and that, too, became a battle to see who was the hungrier. We were not bathed, brushed, nor tended to when injured.

On the first day of the fifth week, Seven, Eight, and I were moved to separate cages; these were slightly larger, but again devoid of shade or protection from the elements. On the way to my own cage I managed to rip a good portion of Daryl's right thumb from the rest of his body. I was beaten profusely over the incident, but I look on it now as one of my finer moments. Sour flesh ripped from such a rancid soul has never tasted as sweet.

For the next seven years I lived, if you could call it that, in those cages. Every two or three weeks, I was hauled off to a covert location and forced to fight other dogs. I dare say I became somewhat of a celebrity. People would cheer at the sight of me, and other dogs would cower. The only pleasure I took in those fights was the excuse to expunge whatever anger and frustration I had amassed towards Daryl. I never enjoyed hurting the other dogs; *they* were worth their salt, had souls, and in different circumstances, they might have added value to the world—polar opposites to the humans which placed them in the arenas with me. I considered the death I dealt as a kind of gift from me to the other dogs, and I respected each one of them. The other owners…they were the ones I'd have loved to have gotten into the pits. Humans are fragile things when unarmed and rarely brave even when they are. I have never once met one who had the same heart and courage as the dogs which I defeated. Not once. *Not even close.*

On my eighth birthday, to the day in fact, serendipity shined on me. That morning I would wage my best, my most valiant, and my last war. A new round of fights had been scheduled and Daryl lumbered about, preparing his "inventory" for travel. He gasped and wheezed as he rolled the cages into his truck, occasionally stopping to engage in a violent coughing fit. It was a revolting sound. But while all of this happened, I managed a trick. I slipped my muzzle! He either did not notice, or didn't care since I would remain inside the cage until there were more humans about to assist in subduing me.

When my mobile prison was rolled to the bottom of the truck's ramp, a loose wheel snapped, and the entire enclosure thundered over. It was a hard enough impact to badly damage one corner of the unkempt frame, and I managed to wrestle out—dazed, but free of the now tangled metal mess.

I have never fought an easier war than the one I waged on Daryl that beautiful day. I inflicted one ghastly wound after another, injuries which I am delighted to say have never healed completely. When I stop in to torture Daryl these days, as I quite often do, I always smile to see him limp and wince as he hobbles about. His left eye is missing now, a good portion of his right calf is gone, and the remaining bits of thumb which I missed as a pup are forever lost to him. Needless to say, he never collected on any more bets.

I know, I know! I can hear your thoughts as you read this, and I do apologize. I would be delighted to expound on the nature of Daryl's gruesome injuries, but I do understand that not all of my readers are as accustomed to such horrible descriptions of violence and agony. For that reason, I will refrain as best I can on the vivid depictions so many of you might find unsettling. I also know that many of you would thoroughly enjoy them, and trust me when I agree that I too wish I could have done more, but Daryl found his courage that day in the shape of a rather large handgun and ended our one-sided battle in fine cowardice form.

Perhaps, dear reader, you now understand my lack of prophetic dying words. Dickens would have been wonderful, as I'm sure you would agree, but at the time, "Mmmpfh," seemed just as noble.

This Dog's Afterlife
Book 2
Available Soon

Made in the USA
Coppell, TX
03 May 2021